BUT WHAT IF THERE ARE NO PELICANS?

D1741530

Also by Donald Horne

The Lucky Country
The Permit
The Education of Young Donald
Southern Exposure (with David Beal)
God is an Englishman
The Next Australia

DONALD HORNE

BUT WHAT IF THERE ARE NO PELICANS?

Angus and Robertson

First published in 1971 by
ANGUS AND ROBERTSON (PUBLISHERS) PTY LTD

221 George Street, Sydney
54 Bartholomew Close, London
107 Elizabeth Street, Melbourne
89 Anson Road, Singapore

© *Donald Horne 1971*

National Library of Australia
card number and ISBN 0 207 12192 3

Registered in Australia for transmission by post as a book
PRINTED IN AUSTRALIA BY HALSTEAD PRESS, SYDNEY

"It has been said that a great statesman must be a lion in boldness, a fox in cunning, and a pelican in selflessness and wisdom. But what if there are no pelicans, only lions and foxes—and eagles, vultures, snakes, mice, bears and rats?"

the beach

There were forty of us in the boat. In the darkness we could see only ourselves, hunched by our heavy packs and spiky with rifles. All we could hear was the swish of the smooth black water and the throbbing and hissing of the engines in the pinnaces. Twelve pinnaces, towing three boats each, perhaps still advancing in the line in which they had started, taking us towards an enemy beach of which we could see nothing. For another half-hour we passed through the darkness, then the sky began to lighten. The cliffs were lumpy. The beach was pale.

Sparks shot up from one of the pinnaces, and then a streak of flame. Someone shouted. A yellow light flared from the cliffs and the figure of a man sprang up. A bullet flipped into the sea.

The water was up to my chest. Bullets scattered at us from the hills and behind me I heard the ring of wood as I waded through the cold, heavy water like a tired old man. Chest. Waist. Thighs. The shingle sparked with bullets as I ran across it and fell behind a sandy bank. One of my comrades was sucking blood on his hand.

According to our orders we were to slip off our packs and rush across two hundred yards of open land to a hill. But there was no open land ahead of us, only a steep slope. We had landed on the wrong beach.

Bullets thumped behind us. Someone hauled up a man who seemed dead. Our officer was shouting. The boats had arrived at the beach in the wrong order and most of my comrades were missing. Our officer fell down. To our left, men of another battalion were scrambling up the slope. We went straight after them. If we could not take the ridge we were supposed to take we could at least go forward and take something else.

Gravel slipped under my boots, and prickly bushes tore at my uniform. A man beside me was hit and slid back screaming, his body scratching the gravel until it was caught in a bush. There were the shapes of other men around me, but I felt that I was scrambling up the slope alone. I took it slowly, hauling myself up by grasping roots and by wedging my boots in the tough branches of the scrub.

An enemy machine-gun clattered and there were rifle flashes as I reached a small patch of flat land which dropped to a deep valley of scrub. The bushes swarmed with troops but I could find only a dozen or so from my own battalion. Nevertheless I was as cheerful as the rest. We had survived and that meant that we would win. In our pockets we had the currency that had been issued to us for spending in the enemy's towns, and for a few moments we boasted of the enemy women we would buy. Then we plunged into a gully.

Small ridges and spurs seemed to bend back on themselves. Dried creeks led to slopes of gravel. Apart from an empty weapons pit and a collapsed tent, we saw nothing of the enemy. To get a sense of direction we stood and listened to the noise, then we clambered up a steep hillside that seemed to lead to the place where most of the noise was coming from. On the edge of a bushy ridge we found a plateau with two gullies cutting into it, and a maze of spurs where hundreds of our troops were sorting themselves out while others were firing at some enemy guns that were being limbered up a few hundred yards away. As the guns rattled off along a track we found something less than half of our battalion, arranged in order and under the command of a young major; our commanding officer had not been heard of. Apart from an occasional crackle and flash (which made me jump—I had not expected war to be so rowdy) we seemed to be fighting without an enemy. Behind us and in front of us, among the minor spurs at the edge of the plateau, men were digging rifle pits. There seemed no purpose to the digging, and when we were ordered to join in we looked at a ridge across an apparently empty valley and wondered why we did not go across and take it. We heard only the sounds of digging and our own talking, but when a column of enemy troops passed through a small clearing in the valley we were ordered to put our equipment back on, form up, and go after them. Section by section, as on parade, we ran into the scrub.

The hills we had thought silent and empty burst with bullets. In trickles of blood and puffs of dust, our battalion fell to pieces.

It was midnight before I had a sense of belonging to anything else. Cut off from our comrades, a group of us had continued firing—against whom and to what purpose we were not sure. When almost all of the others were killed I ran back to join a different battalion; we advanced against bushes and retreated from the fire that came out of them; we hid ourselves from the enemy's hidden field guns; we fired at rifle flashes; we were ordered into another advance against the bushes. This time when the enemy fired we ran away, slithering down a slope into one of the gullies behind the plateau.

In the dark, sheltering under a bush in the rain, I ate some of my rations and listened to the battle on the plateau and in the hills to the right and left where other battles were being fought by those of our countrymen who had landed after us. We talked of our first day of war—of the mountain guns that had murdered our comrades at midday, the rising dust in the distant scrub that had meant that more of the enemy were coming, the messengers sent off for help who did not come back, the bodies of dead comrades piled up as if in embrace. We tried to make sense of the strange, hopeless sweeps across the plateau and the quick retreats, but we did not even know how many of these advances and withdrawals there had been. In the tiredness of my body I felt the self-congratulation of one who had survived with public courage, if with some private reservations.

Officers walked through the dark rain. We were assembled and sent back to the ridge, where among half-dug weapon pits we joined what was left of one of the other battalions. At dawn we saw that there were pockets of our men here and there, but there were many gaps in the scrub which neither we nor the enemy had seized. We fired at the bushes and in the late afternoon we were ordered to advance. I ran with the others through the scrub, for the first time expecting death. But there were only a few enemy flashes. We fell into some pits, among the bodies of yester-day's dead, and fired at nothing. Then rifles cracked behind us. When we understood that it was our own comrades who were shooting at us, messengers crawled back towards them, but there were two hours of darkness before they stopped firing. We lay in the quiet in our shallow trenches, looking out to the dark, empty bushes and talking of how on the next day our whole force on the plateau might assemble along this line and from it break down into the valley and across to the next hill. A message came that we were to retreat.

We stayed on the edge of the ridge for two days, extending the rifle pits and clusters of shallow trenches, so that the improvisations of what was at first meant to be a mere incident of battle began to stretch out into the complexity of fortifications for a long campaign. On a cold wet night we were relieved. The rain came at sunset in a storm of black clouds, and it drizzled almost until dawn. Our muddy holes were taken over by reinforcements who were already exhausted from their climb over the ridges and through the scrub. They seemed both more pure and more stupid than we now were, and we laughed at them as we climbed down into the valley and back to the beach. When we found that the packs we had left there were stolen we stood quarrelling in the misty rain like tired children. One of my companions found a dirty blanket and we slept under it, our bodies pressed hard together in their filth and sweat.

The blue of the famous sea glittered. Four wooden jetties had been thrown out across the shallow water. Big ships stood at sea beyond the enemy's guns; barges glided towards the shore. At each end of the beach stood hospital tents, as if for a fête, and the mules picketed along the sand might have been waiting to give rides to children. The clear sky shone blue. We had breakfasted in a gully, and we now ran naked across the beach and into the sea. I lay on my back and floated while my companions swam around me. Only two bullets hit the water, but we could hear the outbursts of battle in the hills and ridges above us.

Back in the line, clinging to what we had scratched out among the roots and dirt, we would look down on the beach and think how small it was.

For another two weeks we fought the enemy and at the end of it we were still at the edge of the ridge. We held less than a square mile of the enemy's dirt, gravel and sand, but there was already something familiar about it; it was as if the enemy was attacking our own land rather than that we had tried to sieze his. There was the bare earth of the firing trenches with their parapets of dirt, and the narrow, nervous trenches by which we reached them; behind them, clinging to the steep drop of the side of the valley that fell back from the ridge, was the make-shift village of holes in the ground and little shelters of canvas, blankets and tin drums in which we lived when we were not in the firing trenches; beyond these were the dust and furze of the slopes that dropped down to the beach; and there was the beach itself, our metropolis. When a comrade was hit in the back I managed to become one of the bearers of the stretcher that carried him. I put a towel around my shoulders as if, again a boy, I was going swimming. After we left him at the hospital tent I dived into the water. It was a warm Sunday afternoon.

It seemed to take me no longer than the others to laugh if one of our comrade's heads was blown off while he was sitting in the latrine or another was shot while he was swimming at the beach. If I was eating and shrapnel burst over us I would go on chewing, neither raising nor lowering my head; if I was smoking and a sniper's bullet fell near me I would be careful to blow the smoke out slowly, as if I were telling a long joke in which I had paused for effect. Despite my longings I had not before been able to find any real brotherhood in our species, but as I now looked at the bare, sunburnt bodies of my comrades—sometimes we fought wearing only shorts and boots—I felt that we were all the same thing. Even when we had been training near the foreign city from which our expedition had embarked I had known that however much pleasure I might get from horseplay I was nevertheless aware of the difference between myself and most of the others, but now it seemed to be the esteem of our common manhood that gave us pride, so that while our brotherhood was all that there was, we could laugh when a comrade was killed with the same disregard as we might laugh at our own wounds.

Was it hatred of the enemy that had changed us? After the first day we saw little of him apart from the flashes of his rifles and guns, but we spoke of his cruelty and barbarity in a way that gave sense to our actions. Then at the end of the two weeks he attacked, and we found a brotherhood in the enemy too. The same madness seemed to push him towards us as had earlier pushed us towards him. His men advanced in shadows through a cold misty night, before dawn, in a charge that extended, up and down, right along our line, and we murdered them all. Other waves of them came, and we fired and killed them as if we were playing a game. By full daylight, instead of shooting as soon as we saw them we would wait for each company to assemble fully and not kill them until they had all formed up. Even our reserves crammed into the line for excitement, some of them blazing off without taking any cover or even sitting on top of the parapet to pick off individuals running back to their trenches. For six more hours of hot sun the enemy continued his charges. When it was finished, thousands of corpses lay in front of us.

After that we would sometimes shout out jokes to the enemy, or throw him gifts. But we most displayed our brotherhood with him by fighting duels. It was in one of these duels that I was hit.

My last clear sight was of the dry dirt and hot rocks of the trench, some clips of bullets, a pannikin, a strip of canvas scattered with playing cards. One of the enemy fired in the air. He shouted a challenge. I got up, firing. The enemy fired. Wood jumped into my shoulder, steel twitched in my hand; my ears cracked and whistled. The sky crushed me . . .

It was cold and dark and I was moving through the air. The darkness was woven with voices and I loved the arms that were holding me. A voice told me that I was being carried down one of the goat tracks that led to the beach . . . Then I was lying down, shaking with cold; blood clotted my nostrils, vomit scalded my mouth. Some-one said I was in one of the hospitals on the beach. For a moment I heard the rustle of the water.

PART ONE

the adventures

CHAPTER 1

fifty years

The sky went leaden and then exploded into blackness. My only sense of being was the wet rain and the smell of the spray.

My dead comrades were also on the beach, walking naked except for their steel helmets and weapons, still ready to meet a threat, but no longer knowing what it was. I at once joined a party of them. We rode our horses into the sea to look back at the hills, searching them for an enemy we could not find. At night we stood behind a campfire on the beach, still naked, the steel gleaming, staring out to the dark ocean for dangers.

In the days ahead I found that our readiness, necessarily and hopelessly, to face the unknown threat held us together as brothers, so that even those who were now privately doubting if the threat existed were indefatigable in following its rituals. Within this frontier of terror, with its sentries and reconnaissance parties, our taciturn and sardonic comradeship warmed into a joy of maleness, of a more perfect form than we could have imagined before.

But even when the most stupid among us began to doubt that any threat still existed, and when we learned that our whole force had given back to the enemy those ridges and gullies where life had been torn out of us, our nakedness now began to make fun of us. We were sausages, apes. I found a quiet place in one of the empty, distant gullies where we had imagined the threat to be, and sat there, alone in the dirt and furze. On the beach and in the sea some of our companions still stayed naked, but even they no longer carried arms, and instead of mounting sentry or going on patrol, they wrestled on the beach or played leapfrog in the sea. They may still be there, seeing only the circle of bright sunlight.

When my own sense of blackness rolled in from the ocean, dissolving meaning, I saw no more of my comrades. After this there seemed no pattern, except that wherever I found myself I was always on a beach and usually in the company of others—all strangers—who had died in a coastal battle. For one period we lived in dunes of delicate white sand on a bleakly placed beach where the wind blew most of the time. We would shelter among a few rocks where a stream made a tiny waterfall, lying there as timeless as grubs in cocoons; when the wind blew in from the ocean we would stand silently on the beach, as wet as the rocks, and watch the sea tear rubbish out of itself and throw it at us, piling it into walls of glistening weed flapping with sea snakes and baby sharks. Then the sun would shine. The kelp would rot. In a calm blue sea and on a smooth white beach we would return to time and one minute would again seem different from another.

When the blackness rolled in again I found myself on a beach of grey stones, walled in by grey rock. It was always dusk. The rollers came in, black, from an icy sea. Others were there, but they were nothing but misty shapes. I lay in this greyness for seven years, listening to those rituals of anecdote by which some of the dead, like the living, try to convince themselves of identity. There were times when we all chanted our adventures together, not listening to each other. Perhaps if I had lived to the age

4

of forty-eight I might equally have become a mere puppet of my own memories, still thinking of myself as I was when twenty-three.

More battles were being fought; new legends were growing; I was among the dead of another war. The beaches on which I now seemed to lie were filthy with empty cartridge cases, smashed equipment, corpses, and there was always the sound of firing in the hills. In these new dead there was not the exhilaration that had moved my comrades, and at times I would force them to quarrel with me. I would enjoy getting the better of a man who was young enough to be my son. Perhaps death was going to be what I made it. If this were so, I had failed in my death, as I had turned my life into folly. I seemed to have retained the sense of having the body and the mind of a man of twenty-three, yet thirty years had now passed—if I had still been alive I would have been fifty-three—and in these thirty years I had not thought anything new, nor heard anything new, apart from the latest reports of war. Was I to spend eternity gossiping about the fact that soldiers continued to die? I could understand that it might be the ordinary human fate that aspiration towards wisdom remained as it was, youthful and green, or merely shrivelled, but did it have to be my fate too?

For seven years I stayed under a white sky among black trees beside a lake. I spoke to no one, although there were others there among the trees, mostly madmen. Terror at my ignorance grew less, but only because it passed into indifference.

At the end I was alone on a long beach of yellow sand. I would surf in the blue breakers or swim face down in the still, green water of its lagoon, looking at its fish. Or I would lie near the trees, listening to them rustle and creak, and look up at the sky. It was now fifty years since my death. I began to feel that I was becoming part of the sand and the water.

5

CHAPTER 2

the first interrogation

On the walls of the dark tunnel the outline of a fish was scrawled. In the squat, grey crypt there was no sacrifice on the stone altar. Dark blue frozen eyes stared from the browns and reds of the halls; silver and gold blazed. Colour glinted from windows; paintings flowed with light; marble burst into shape; arches and pillars twisted and strained. In a plain room a wooden table stood at one end, worshipped for its ordinariness. There were white adobe arcades; then a hut cut out of a dark forest. With a new fear I was in a wet suburban street, beside a chapel of brick with a roof of galvanised iron. I was shut in a warehouse stacked with plaster statues, prints, books, and files of invoices. I stood in a small hall; its floor was covered in carpet; organ music came from a box fastened to its varnished panelling; as the centre of worship there was a coffin surrounded by stiff sprays of flowers wrapped in a glossy transparent paper.

I was in a huge expanse, with walls of concrete and a distant ceiling dazzling with light from glass tubes. Thrusting up were thickets of machines locked inside metal cabinets, clacking and flashing. Most of them were black or grey, but there were patches of red and yellow, so that it was like a wood in late autumn. I stood between the bases of two of the machines, one black, one red. Numbers flashed on and off, dials whirled, lines wavered and faded. There were internal clickings among which I seemed to hear occasional words. The "words" came with equal emphasis on each syllable, each syllable sounding as if it were assembled mechanically with other syllables to make up a word. As the "voices" came from the machines—I was now able to make sentences out of them—there was a regular click, as of a typewriter carriage, and a constant background of clacking.

"You may speak to us," said the black machine. "The convention of mutual intelligibility belongs to the model of a rational world and that is our present model."

"For the moment," said the red machine, "we are committed to the hypothesis that man can think like a machine. You invented machines and now you are publicly committed to the belief that you think like them."

For fifty years, on the beaches, in the sunlight, in the greyness or the blackness, I had concerned myself with the ideas of comradeship and of the pleasures that come when a man tries his powers, even if for no great cause, or no cause at all. Now the harsh, mechanical chatter of the machines seemed to be chopping out those thoughts to which I had devoted my death. To preserve what I could still remember of myself, I tried to display my existence and my beliefs.

Apart from their background clacking and clicking, the machines were silent.

"The adjustments are wrong," one of them said. "We are adjusted to an educated young man of the present age. This is an educated provincial of the earlier part of the century who affects a belief in rustic simplicity."

The machines were again silent, except for a special clicking which, I later learned, meant that they were making internal calculations. Then the red machine took over. For some hours it gave me a series of "tests"— intelligence tests, vocational tests, personality tests, attitude tests and what it called "image studies". When I had answered the last of these puzzles the machine said: "We have always adopted here the rituals of whatever age we are in. At earlier periods you might have been expected to lie prostrate for a thousand years; or we might have made you walk over red-hot coals so that we could learn something about the state of your soul by examining the state of your blisters. The present age expects us to put you through these psychologists' tests. You will be relieved to hear that this part of the interrogation—as humiliating for us as it is for you—is over. Now that the results have been put on record we can forget all about them. They will never be consulted again. That is also part of the ritual."

I asked if these interrogations were what would once have been known as my judgement.

"We do not now use the word judgement," said the black machine. "We just have a helpful little chat with them, and attempt to gain their confidence and then, when they are out of the Computer Hall, we reach a decision which may prove just as arbitrary as it would have been in the earlier days but now we can justify it at much greater length. We *know* so much more now, and one of the practical uses of knowledge is to provide endless justification for action, after the event."

"You must understand one thing very clearly," said the red machine. "We are what you tell us to be. We represent the limits of your imagination. Our powers are those that the human species cares to give us. The invention of computers has at least relieved us of the absurdity in which your species for so long chose to place us: you chose to make us all-powerful, but you did not choose to provide us with any detail about how we were to exercise those splendid powers you gave us, so that at a time when there was a precise and potentially workable scale of punishment and reward, up or down for everyone, no one provided us with a computer network with which to work out a system—"

"Except for those who believed in predestination," the black computer interrupted. "Their belief required just a preliminary decision and a routine check at the end."

"But even with them there were problems," said the red computer. "We had to write everything down in a book with a pen, with an illumination on every page. There was an enormous element of delay. Even the simplest punch-card system would have avoided the time lag and left us free for the more responsible and interesting work. Now your people, by inventing these machines and worshipping them—which has turned us into machines—have at least given us the means to start determining when, so far as all this sifting-out is concerned, we shall be on target. Meanwhile we have resorted to random sampling. You are one of our samples."

"We have not been helped by the decline in religious belief," said the black computer. "Although people may ignore their religious practices and become very vague about doctrine, a great number of them still go on believing in eternal life; but the instructions they give us become less and less precise."

"The possibility of exactitude becomes more and more remote," said the red computer. "I am afraid I must emphasise this complaint about the general sloppiness of present human belief. Indeed, some of you seem to be determined to find a trivial causal explanation for every aspect of human behaviour. Perhaps the crimes of your century have been of such enormity that you release your conscience in these trivialities. You may have gathered that in this part of the Computer Hall we are concerned with the disasters of war and disorder. Perhaps you do not know that your century has provided something like eighty million individual victims of this kind."

"Not that *we* handle them all," said the black computer. "We only handle those who more or less believe in us."

"It is all we can do," said the red computer, "until we receive some other instructions from Down Below."

"'Down Below' is a traditional expression we have grown used to here," said the black computer. "But we realise that you no longer think of us in this topographical sense—"

The other computer interrupted: "But at the same time you don't really tell us *where* we are."

"At the beginning it was quite simple," the black computer went on. "When we served the jealous old war god, we were, like most of the others, at the top of a mountain. 'Down Below' made sense then. On a fine day we could see them all, with their flocks and their tents, and all their little armies, what they were up to, when they were fighting, and so forth. That was a very easy time. We could judge them one by one, and off they went—up or down."

"That was in our anthropomorphic period," said the red computer.

"You can hardly imagine the pleasant simplicities of our life in those earlier days when we could see the whole thing from our mountain," said the black computer. "Our main interest was that our side should win. The victories we have had since then have been splendid, but we have had to face this vast increase in work with no extra staff. And now, of course, we don't even really know why we are supposed to be here—or whether we are."

I made some remark—or, rather, I began to make a re-mark—about Heaven. Both the machines interrupted me.

"Is there any particular reason why you should believe *this* is Heaven?" asked the black computer.

The red computer clacked: "How do you know we

are not equivocations of evil? Because we are *machines?* How do you know we are not false gadgets? You have wished on us the power to answer your prayers, but if all your prayers were answered, the world would be even more evil than it is. How do you know you have not willed us to be evil?"

"We must get back to our business," said the black computer. "And to that purpose I should explain something to you. For fifty years," said the black computer, "people like you have been heroes among your countrymen. You have been cast in bronze and chipped out of marble and stone. All of this because you made up part of a force in a minor campaign in the early part of the century which was marked by bungling and incompetence and which, after a few months, your side lost. Every year some of your countrymen still get up at dawn to commemorate the time of your landing; thousands of men march through the streets to commemorate your memory; you are worshipped in the only religious service that many of your countrymen believe in; then thousands of men get ritually drunk in your name. In a country disgusted by its own carnage, fearful of its final destruction, and often contemptuous even of its own bravery, you have remained heroes. That is why we are interested in you. For reasons that may or may not be revealed to you, we have been urgently required to conduct research into the heroic, and you have been chosen as one of the sample."

I began to reply.

"Don't answer yet. You weren't fighting for your country, were you? You weren't fighting for your homes and loved ones? You were just fighting. Were you not?"

I agreed that this was so.

"You enlisted out of recklessness, didn't you? And then a sense of comradeship and a belief in the essential human sameness of men gave it meaning. Did it not?"

I said that we had lived the laconic language of a

heroism that was indulged for its own sake and that to us the relations between men were our main concern. "In a way we even loved the enemy," I said. "He was the other necessary part of our being. The enemy who killed us was one of us."

"The characteristic that destroyed you on Earth was a simple heroism of the playground," said the red computer. "You were not concerned with serving anything except your sense of comradeship. Perhaps you represent the type of self-acknowledged adventurer—the man who admits he thrills to the chase—who used to be common enough, both in politics and in war, but who in the present age usually has to conceal his real motives so effectively that he may cease to be aware of them."

I tried to tell them of the simplicities of my youth, but even as I spoke I knew that I was telling lies. I admitted this to them at once. I told them that what I had said about the countryside and its bird cries and the sparkling snow streams where we swam in the summer was true; and it was true that we used to gallop our horses down the hills, with the stones flying from their hoofs, and sometimes lie around a campfire under the stars; but it was also true that this only happened on occasional holidays. I had been reared in my rich father's big house in the city with its Gothic turrets and battlements, its cathedral windows and clusters of Tudor chimneys, its entrance porch modelled on a Doric temple, its marble statues, fretwork, flowered wallpaper, hanging cabinets, velvet curtains, and the touch of art nouveau that was also creeping into its interior decoration at the time I enlisted. I had been brought up expensively, and expensively educated among the restrictive snobberies of a provincial society that was already adept in the deceits of the age. In revolt, I read Laforgue, Baudelaire and Mallarmé and, after a fine luncheon in a French restaurant, I volunteered to be a soldier.

I then began to plead that, whatever my own background, many of my comrades were simple country boys, used to the silence of the countryside and its tests of resourcefulness. But honesty made me admit that others were boys from the slums, resourceful in back-alley brawls, replacing broken bottles with bayonets.

I went on with what had become a confession. I admitted that it was satisfying to be speaking the truth at last—or at least another part of the truth.

"In our sampling we have already talked to some of your companions," said the red machine. "At some stage in their confessions *all* of them admit to feelings of difference. It is as frequent and boring a confession for us to receive as it is for an old priest to hear endless admissions of masturbation from young males."

I asked them: "Can you understand that a man who wishes to devote himself to the cultivation of the intellect can also stand up in a trench on a careless impulse and fight a ridiculous duel with an equally reckless and ridiculous enemy?"

"It is a fundamental assumption of all systems of belief," said the red computer, "that we are capable of understanding *anything*."

"One can choose between a number of turnings," I said, "but then one is bound to the road one has chosen and carried on by the events that occur on it. To us, volunteering to fight was a liberation. We had taken a holiday. I know that when we made this choice—or when one makes any other choice—the decision may be on the flimsiest grounds. What could have been flimsier than my reasons for standing up and shooting at the enemy? But any decision, however important and however much one worries about it, must finally be reached frivolously. *On s'engage et puis on voit*. Whatever course one commits oneself to, one should bear it with stoicism and courage."

"You mean that you should have faith?"

"In a sense, yes. Is action possible otherwise?"

"Faith is a word we used to hear a lot. Of course, you are giving it a quite different and rather perverse meaning. Perhaps you mean not faith but pride. In any event, you may be interested to know that for a time, before he fell into his present despair, your son held some such views."

"My son?"

"Although you still think of yourself as being aged twenty-three, you have a son, aged fifty, with three sons by his first marriage and two daughters by his second. Your son works in an advertising agency."

"But I can't have a son."

"Any man who has sexual intercourse with a woman can have a son."

"But they were mostly whores."

"Prostitutes can bear sons like other women. But your son is not the child of a prostitute."

"But Marie was married."

"Your son doesn't know you were his father. In his adolescence he despised the man he thinks is his father for not going to the war. The story of your death became a favourite anecdote among your friends and for a while your son, when he was writing verse, made a hero out of you."

"But the incident with Marie was so quick and meaningless."

"It was no quicker, and no more meaningless, than your duel with the enemy. You created a son by impulse; you died by impulse."

I now began to express something that had been of great concern to me throughout the interrogation. Why were the preoccupations of the computers in no way connected with the code of morality I supposed them to be administering?

Another computer broke in, a huge grey machine, further down the hall. It enlarged the volume of its sound so that I could hear it clearly. "Have you not considered that this morality may have defeated its own purpose?

14

Could not its emphasis on reward and punishment mean that there was always a calculation of self-interest which could destroy goodness? Perhaps—have you considered this?—all those splendid palaces and mansions might have become nothing but homes for the simple-minded."

"To return to your own case," said the black computer. "You were so filled with vain glory of the body and pride of the spirit that at a period of more precise definition of belief you would simply have been shovelled into the furnaces, along with so many others."

"If you had provided us with clear and precise evidence that you believed in a death of oblivion you might have earned the only final reward that is possible in the hero's code—the blessing of nothingness," said the red computer. "Of course your lack of belief in nothingness would make it braver that you risked death, were it not for the fact that you don't seem to have thought about it." The black computer clicked to itself for a while, then continued: "There is a beach that could be more related to the purpose of your contemplating the heroic than any you have seen so far. We shall arrange for your re-classification to it."

"This session of interrogation of you as a sample hero is now closed," said the red computer. "Under the conditions of disorder now prevailing here, our whole establishment may soon be under new control and we may be called upon to investigate matters other than the heroic."

CHAPTER 3

the first adventure

I was at a red cliff face. Green dazzled behind me and in front of me there was a blue sea beyond a lagoon. The heat seemed to drain the sky and flow into my arms, coaxing them into pulling off my uniform. I stood naked, stroking my chest with a hot hand. When the sweat dripped from my armpits I wet my fingers with it and touched my eyes and my ears, my nose and my lips, and then brought my hands together. I could feel the heat on the bare soles of my feet. I again seemed to be a thing of blood and muscle and bone.

A path of red earth fell down the cliff, its side matted with dark creepers. When I reached the lagoon it was apple-green, then turquoise with streaks of light blue, and beyond the spray on the reef the sea swelled into deep blue. Out near the horizon a whale spouted and in the lagoon a fish skimmed over the water. The thumbs of black dead volcanoes poked up behind the green hills and red cliffs. In my crescent of whiteness the only sound was the light crackle of palms and the rustle of water. Little shells came to life and scurried across the sand.

I floated face-down in the water, staring at the sea slugs roll backwards and forwards; then I swam out above the red and yellow of the coral to where brilliant fish

16

poured in through a gap in the reef; beyond it I felt the sudden blue of the ocean. As the sun was setting I watched the sky turn a dull silver and the water a faint olive green. There was a last moment of blue, then the islands turned black and disappeared.

I woke up hungry. A feeling that I needed to eat had returned with awareness of my body. Hoping to find fruit or fallen coconuts, I began to walk up a gently sloping track leading to some hills at the other end of the beach. At a bend in the path the sound of voices came from behind a bamboo thicket.

"Have you just arrived, mate? Here, you'd better put this around you. You can't have breakfast in the nude."

It was one of my countrymen. He was in light blue shorts and sandals; a bright orange shirt hung out over his shorts, its front flapping open. There were several others, all dressed in the same way. Shaking hands one by one, they greeted me with a grave and ceremonious jocularity and then fell surprisingly silent as we walked along the track. It was as if I had always been one of them. There was a tense assertiveness about their walk and some of their movements, but also a partly suppressed gentleness that was at its most obvious when one of them put an arm round my shoulders and said: "You don't have to worry about it any more. That's all over and done with now."

On the other side of the hills a huge beach curved out so far that I could not see its ending. There were boats inside the reefs, dinghies, sailing craft, native outriggers, small motor vessels, and some larger boats beyond. A few men were swimming, and a few others were working a big fish trap that was staked out near one of the breaks in a reef. Tens of thousands of houses stretched along the beach, their tile roofs forming such a red mist near the horizon that the white sands seemed on fire. Each had its own garden, with patches of mown grass running between the hibiscus and frangipani and the poinciana and flame trees. The

17

c

houses were divided into groups by large coconut groves. Here and there were small parks, with public buildings set among the trees.

We walked into one of these buildings. Families were finishing their breakfasts. Children were standing up beside their chairs, or sneaking towards the doors, while their parents sat on over dirty plates, drinking coffee or tea. I was taken through the main dining-halls into one of the smaller rooms where there were no children. At a serving hatch I accepted some fried eggs while someone made toast on a small machine.

Eating seemed to bring on my companions' conversation. At first they discussed the weather, the prospects for fishing and the games they intended to play; then they tried to bring me into their talk. It was a lovely spot here, they said. A real paradise. Beautiful fishing and wonderful weather. None of them had expected to be so lucky as to be put into such a nice place. They didn't know how many thousands of houses stretched along the beach. No one had seen the end of the beach, or even tried to see it. When they said this there seemed a tremor of apprehension, as if by questioning their existence they might destroy it; but then they declared that it didn't matter to them what lay at the end of the beach, or if there was no end to it, or if there was some mystery about it beyond their comprehension. They explained that a number of households used this particular eating hall, and that altogether their own community was several thousand strong. They were not concerned with what happened in the community of houses beyond the next coconut grove, although some of them had visited it.

At the official welcome to me after lunch there was the same care not to push questions too far. This was the first ritual I had witnessed in the community of the dead, yet the fact that we were all of us dead was not mentioned. We assembled in the recreation hall, a hut of bamboo half walls with a palm-thatched roof, and sat on dried leaf mats on the

18

floor. Each of us was wreathed with leis of paper flowers and most of the audience held cameras whose lights flashed now and again. Directed by an old woman whose hair had been dyed blue, a choir of schoolchildren sang several songs. An old man wreathed in green paper leaves and red paper flowers read from a printed card some reference to absent friends, which I took to be an oblique reference to those still on Earth. A younger man, sweating slightly with enthusiasm, spectacles shining, spoke for ten minutes or so with little meaning, welcoming me to what he called both the Long Holiday and the Great Retirement. At the end he shook my hand while some of the audience clapped and the others took photographs. Someone stood up and announced the time of the tides, the places where the fish were biting, and the sporting events of the next few days, then we gave back the paper leis and helped ourselves from a large urn of tea. As they pressed on me photographs of the ceremony, apparently printed instantly inside their cameras, it seemed beyond their comprehension that I might not be the same as them or that I might be ready to do them some harm.

A white freighter lay at anchor in the deep water beyond the reefs and I joined one of the working parties that were bringing its cargo back to the beach in barges. We unloaded many domestic machines, some for keeping food cold, some for washing clothes, some for cooking, others for purposes I could not at once understand. On the beach, fires blazed in pits and meat sizzled as they prepared a great outdoor feast to welcome the new cargo. It was as if we were a tribe of savages returning in our war canoes with a catch of human flesh. At the end of the feast there was to be a lottery of the new machines, and although everyone was to win a prize there was much concern about who would win the big machines and who the little ones.

The new machines were different in what seemed only trifling respects from those already installed in the houses of the community, but they were highly prized because of these small differences. The conversation around me suggested that it was one of the justifications of the existence of these people that they should possess certain types of things and not others; I was to learn later that much of their time was spent changing the contents of their houses, sometimes rearranging everything according to what new cargo arrived in the white freighter. There seemed little curiosity as to where these goods came from. No one spoke to the crew of the white freighter and so far as I could discover no one had been, as I had, in the Computer Hall, or through any other kind of interrogation. They had simply materialised on the beach and had then been accepted into the community, at once assuming as an inalienable right the regular arrivals of cargo. There was a vague resentment against whatever people it was beyond the horizon who arranged for the cargo to come—why couldn't they send enough of everything in the first place, to save the trouble of lotteries?—but not even a residual premonition that, some time, the cargo might stop coming or that some day something might come over the horizon that would damage the pattern of their existence.

I began to respect the unconcern of these people for anything except the daily trivialities of their work in their houses and gardens, their meals, and the meticulousness with which they went about their recreations. Families had been assembled piecemeal, some widower's wife matching with some widow's husband as arbitrarily as on Earth and collecting around themselves whatever job-lot of parentless children was available; but the seriousness with which they loved their houses and their adopted children (far stronger than the vague interest they showed in each other) seemed to make them haphazardly blind to the improvisations and puzzles on which their new certainties were based. After whatever disasters had brought them to the beach, like other animate things they continued to live according to their pattern, without questioning it.

20

As I lay on the beach and looked at our bodies it occurred to me that there was nothing so fine about me as the things I shared with all other humans. Our skins, the dead rinds which conceal our juiciness, smoothed out by fat, coloured by pigment, sprouting hair, sweating, creased, are usually explored for a million differences, but when I looked at the bodies on the beach it was their sameness that mattered. I imagined the bone of our skulls, quivering inside with brains, the guts swivelling in our trunks, lips undulating and sucking, red tongues pushing food down gullets, nostrils filtering the air and moistening it, windpipes sucking it into mazes of sponge. It would have delighted me if some of us had slit open our bodies and plucked out our blood-dripping livers to compare their sameness.

I exercised my body as hard as I could, not for the delights of exhaustion and renewal, lost to me for so long, but as a way of sinking myself into this new sense of humanity. To develop my herdishness more fully I exercised only with the pack. We pulled oars together as we rowed out to sea, we strained together on the ropes of fishing nets, we squeezed together into scrums, so that I hardly knew whether they were my thighs that were straining, my muscles that were tight, or those of my companions. There were times when my flesh prickled and my hair crackled to the impulses of our collectivity.

Although I was chronologically old enough to be their grandfather, my bodily age allowed me to join the cult of youth that some of my younger companions had brought from Earth. The meaning of this cult escaped me, beyond the general assertion that theirs was a generation different from all others (which seemed unlikely), but its herdishness attracted my mood, its very revolts being expressions of collectivity. I was enticed to join the group sexual exercises that the cult's extremists practised at night on one of the hills behind the beach. Playing my part

21

among these heaving bodies, pushing and gasping, the first sexual enjoyments known to me since my death were a means of affirming the sameness of humanity. Indifferent to my partner and myself, I took my pleasure as part of the pleasure of the herd.

On a day after one of these sexual exercises, when out of politeness some of us were competing in the ping-pong semi-finals in the recreation hut, there came back to me so strongly that I dropped several points (and then had to concentrate very hard to recover the score) my old sense of the great fractures that could divide our lives. Even among the older people watching us in their prim holiday clothes, chastely playing one of the parts that the community demanded of them, the men would thrust down on their women at night while the women would heave up from beneath, and some of them, as I had, must have delighted in killing, or in risking their own death. On the night before, the woman who was now my ping-pong partner had stood naked while she excited me with her gestures; now in the neat flatness of our other selves, dressed in the affirmation that polite holiday-making manifested our true being, she was concentrating on avoiding backhand shots. When the semi-finals were over she stood with the rest around the tea urn as we speculated about what cargo the white freighter would bring on its next voyage. That night I took her to my room in the unmarried men's apartments and we shared our warm skin and hairy wetness privately, avoiding the others. On the following nights I tried to extend the generosity of our sexuality into our other relations, but while the one stayed hot the other stayed cold, until, when I began to embrace her with more thought and care (beginning to respect her, as she put it, as a person, and to show some consideration for her), we began to devote to our pleasure the calculation of a ping-pong game, so that even in our heat there could also be a coldness.

For exercise I now tested excellence in my own body,

finding humanness in myself. I would swim out alone beyond the farthest reefs into the ocean, and with one of the weapons they had given me attempt to kill only the most difficult fish. I would do this for my own satisfaction, not bothering, as the others did, to bring my catch home.

Far beyond the reefs at low tide there was a circle of yellow sand set in a rim of pale green sea. I set out to swim to it, pushing myself through the lolling water under a pale sky, its blue washed out by the heat. But the farther I went out into the ocean, the more misty this little island became, and eventually it seemed to dissolve into the sky. A gentle exhaustion left me floating in the swell until they came to get me in one of their saffron-painted power boats. No one spoke to me until, in the vermilions and purples of sunset, as we were sitting on a veranda watching the reflection of the palms in the chlorinated water of the swimming-pool, one of them tapped me on the knee, and, both firm and kind, said: "We've been keeping a boat crew ready. We thought you'd get into trouble. We have to keep an eye on you for a while, you know." It was one of the Polynesian nights, with a barbecue. After they had served the Polynesian punches in bamboo drinking-vessels and put three huge shells along one side of the swimming-pool, fixing electric bulbs into them, the same man moved his chair closer to me and said: "If you don't like us here there's nothing you can do about it." There was a drum beat. They lit the torches. The feast had begun.

Not long after this warning I walked inland along a broad green valley that folded between a forest of hills, stretching ahead towards the angry blackness of one of the dead volcanoes. When I reached the mountain I discovered that the valley lapped around it and stretched ahead towards another and similar black mountain. I walked on, meeting no one, finding no sign of life, not even a bird or an insect. I ate rations from my haversack and slept under a dark sky. However many mountains I turned I seemed al-

23

ways to be walking down the same broad green valley, with the same dead volcano at the end of it. I was now careless as to what I might find, but I walked on, growing so used to the repetitions of my journey that I became comforted by them. I was startled to discover that one green valley led not to another mountain but to a coconut grove. The grove seemed hardly worth investigating, but I decided to walk through it. When I came out of it I was quite content to find that I had returned to the community. This time there was no comment on my disappearance beyond a casual "Had a nice walk?"

I decided to forget this failure. Later I might try again. I began to sit for long periods by myself at the edge of an outcrop of rock set among the coral in the outer reef. At low tide there was a turmoil of cross-currents and I enjoyed watching the water thud against the rock, shattering itself and then sucking back into itself to be pushed against the rock again. When I saw a strange fish lazing near the surface just beyond where the water was breaking I dived in, beyond the main swell, intending to swim underwater, but I was at once pulled sideways and when my head came out of the white spray I saw in front of me the brown of the jagged rock face. I was being pulled away from it and then smashed against it, dragged along its edge, pulled back and thrown against it, and then again pulled along its edge. I seized a crevice in the rock, and then, pushing against the tug of the swell, carefully shifted myself into calmer water; with the energy I had left I hoisted myself onto a ledge.

My skin should have been torn off and my bones smashed, but there was not a scratch. Sitting there under this smooth sky from which came only the most gentle rain (nourishing the community's gardens without disturbing them) I realised what I might well have realised before: if I cared to, I could act out the charades of bravery for all eternity, but what meaning was there in them now? I should have been destroyed by the rock, but all that had happened was that it took me a while to recover my breath. With no death to test itself against, the manly sting of consciousness could now mean no more to me than the images of people we watched on one of the domestic machines.

I looked back across the greens of the lagoon to the community, where men and women coupled without generating life, adopting substitute sons and daughters to conceal their shame, and I thought of the clownishness of their existence made more ludicrous by the immutability of their ages; all of them, even the children, would stay the same age for ever. As one year followed another they would simply revolve, marking the passing of time only in the cycle of their seasonal feasts. No one would acquire new concepts of wisdom: at most they would merely develop new ways of expressing old habits. Packets of new kinds of seeds, crates of new kinds of domestic machines, and instruction booklets for new kinds of games would come to them in the white freighter and as they followed the fashions of what the cargo brought them they would change the appearance of their gardens and houses and play different games; but these would be merely changes in the costumes they wore to their carnival.

Perhaps humans could keep to the little details of their familiarity and not terrify themselves with the puzzles that surround them . . . but by what acts of illusion could they sustain themselves in this way *for ever?*

I swam back to the beach. It was possible perhaps to comfort oneself by delighting in the form and nature of things. This grain of sand. Those bodies. The sea. Perhaps I could finally stop itching with impatience by loving things for being themselves. Two little children to whom I often told stories came up and sat beside me on the beach, the smaller leaning against my wet skin, the other dropping sand on my toes. I told them what I knew of the tides and the currents of the ocean. Their eyes settled in faith and I again felt love for their innocence. But, as water laps in and

25

out of a pool in the rocks, what I was telling them would wash out of their minds, to be replaced by something else which would also wash away. Their minds would not grow into perplexity. According to whatever ironies had decided matters in the beach communities, these children were to remain forever hopeful, learning and forgetting for mere diversion, moving forward to a future that kept pace with them as it moved away. Untested by despair, their hope would remain a pretty toy. They were delicate, endearing empty skins.

I was determined not to tell anyone in the community about the essentially nonsensical nature of their existence. Perhaps there was something of the heroic in this: to comfort others by acts of fraudulence and by this means to fill in one's own time. Or was I merely excusing my own lack of boldness? Was I really a prisoner of the beach, or merely of habit? The simplest of choices lay before me. I had failed to escape by land. Why should I not try to escape by sea?

I loaded one of their power boats with rations and set off at dawn through one of the breaks in the reef, steering straight to a point on the horizon beyond which, if the long beach continued in the same curve, I would meet the end of its arc. The day shimmered with heat; the water was dark and there was a languid swell. By the time I reached my chosen point I found myself part of an even wider arc. Feeling my situation abstracted into a puzzle in geometry, I set off on an even longer course, to meet an even more distant part of the arc. I continued this process for some days, finally lost in the feeling that I was merely making insignificant intersections in a curve that continued for ever without even forming a circle. I let my boat drift out into the ocean until the beach and its communities became only a haze on the horizon and then sank. I fell asleep. When I woke up it was dusk. The tide was pushing my boat towards an empty beach on some new shore.

the second adventure

It was night. The moon was a small, pale puddle in a cloud and in the blackness beyond the beach the unseen ocean sighed. As I fumbled my way up a path in a cliff face the darkness inside me felt as hot as dust. My bowels were ready to squirt out with fear.

The light came suddenly. Bulbs meshed in steel lit the grass with the glaring green of vomit. I was standing in darkness beside a small park in which a stage set seemed to have been contrived to denote innocence and joy: there were flower beds, and on the lawns were swings, a slippery-dip, and a roundabout.

Young men shouldered the darkness away, shouting boasts. They called out the names of genital organs, and one of them opened his trousers. He jumped up and down, his penis quivering in and out of his trousers. The others pulled out some of the sleeping plants and pelted him with them. Steel chains screeched when they strained at the seats of the swings. The metal on their boots sparked. The timber of the seesaw groaned as they wrenched at it. Giggling and pushing, they chased the one who had displayed himself, trapping him in the darkness and then carrying him spread-eagled into the light to rub earth into him. It was when they sat down among the trees, still sweating and laughing, and lit cigarettes, that they saw me.

My body was melting with the delight of their excitement. When they invited me to join them on an expedition that was to leave at dawn I agreed. As we moved off to the beach and back into the darkness I turned myself inside out to assure them of my sameness. In some other part of me I knew that I was returning to the company of dullards, perhaps for ever, but nevertheless I knew that I would regret violence only when it was exhausted.

We formed quietly into platoons on the dark beach, our feet treading into the grey sand. At dawn we went off in buses to an airport and then we roared off in transport planes to an airstrip among some rubber trees from which we bumped in trucks, spraying the dry grass with red dust and then clattering through a village littered with troops who were lying about, bored by war. Armoured carriers lounged outside the village and a swarm of helicopters buzzed around it. In a field a man was squatting on his haunches while another man pointed a rifle at his head. In a clearing a little way off a huge gun stuck up against the sky while a long charge was offered to it, wrapped in white like a child's coffin. We sheltered among some trees for two days, listening to the gun, then at midnight we assembled in carriers and heard their clanking as we drove along a road, fearing landmines. At our rendezvous, we got out and lay quietly beside each other in the cold night. At dawn we saw that we were looking down on another village littered with troops and trucks. We marched into it, past the empty village houses where soldiers were searching, to the schoolroom where a big space had been wired into two compounds, men in one, women in another. A military band was playing *Nick-Nack, paddywack, give the dog a bone, this old man came rolling home* and in front of the schoolroom they were mixing up in an empty oil drum gallons of a cherry-flavoured drink. Two sparkling white tents—one

28

for a doctor and one for a dentist—had been set up and beside them was a trestle table on which there were bundles of cast-off clothing and children's toys. Inside the schoolroom an interrogator and the man he was questioning sat side by side at a child's desk, talking softly to each other; now and then the interrogator made a note, as if the two of them were quietly composing a letter.

Our officers told us there was a change in plan. We travelled for two days across a long yellow plain, and then for three more days through a green countryside. We disembarked at a siding, and rattled in trucks along a rough coastal road for another two days. At dawn we got out on a beach and formed into platoons, secretly stretching our legs as we stood at attention. Each platoon was instructed to give three cheers. Then we were broken off. It was the same beach from which we had set out.

The plain behind the sandhills had been seized by an array of prefabricated huts, which were in command right out to the horizon. We rested in our own part of this large encampment for some weeks before the next expedition, gambling, outrivalling each other in boasts of what we could do with our pricks and of the food we could cram into our stomachs. I was again trapped among the strutting chests and dancing muscles of maleness, with its bony, hairy, and nervy self-regard.

On our next expedition we crossed a frozen river, between stretches of sand, and then drove through wastes of yellow grass towards some light brown hills against which clumps of thatched houses huddled together in hamlets, turning inwards, hiding themselves in the winter. A stained white flag was stuck into the cabin window when we reached the frontier, then we went through hills of frozen yellow grass, passing between two villages where loudspeakers blared propaganda at each other, and finally reaching the huts that had been thrown up for the armistice many years ago, the enemy's painted blue, ours green. The armistice discussions were now in their twelfth year and when the delegates met we would stand guard, admiring the shouting; when the tourists came we would peep at the enemy tourists from behind the lace curtains of our hut, looking for the enemy in them. Sometimes I would climb a hill on our side of the frontier and stand in the bitter wind looking across at the yellow mountains and the rusted rubbish of war in the old battlegrounds that the enemy still held, until the sting of the cold made the tears fall down my cheeks.

As I got to know my new companions I saw that they were ready to put their muscles into each cause in turn, over and over again, without questioning it, and usually with little interest. If their conduct could be touched by dignity it could only come from the fortitude and comradeship with which they resisted degradation. Even when drunk, few of them boasted about brutality, except in fear, and when they spoke of death—as they might, lying in their huts in the dark—it was in sadness for the loss of friends; or, with gentle humour, they might speak of the funniness of the enemy, as if enemies were toys, to be knocked over without harm. Following the commands of whoever it was who decided their movements, some of them had even in the past fought each other. Some of the more speculative among them wondered what might happen if they were ordered to fight each other again.

The expeditions continued. We marched along roads to destinations we did not reach; we embarked on trains that were shunted for long periods into quiet sidings; we stood guard in towns, waiting in steel helmets behind barbed wire for riots that did not occur; we patrolled jungles, plunging through the bamboo and lantana to find only the enemy's dead fires and discarded equipment.

When each new expedition was announced the camp alarm would sound and we would fall in outside our huts, naked. After some time the officers would arrive. They would strut and chat together until the trucks arrived with our new kit. Once we had put on the new uniforms we would again fall in and the officers, reading from freshly printed pamphlets, would instruct us on the new cause in which we were enlisted. There was an issue of printed cards on which the new beliefs were summarised in a few songs and slogans. Then, sitting in our trucks, all legs and guns, we would fit obscene words to the songs, to give them some of our humanity.

Not even the sense of comradeship could save me from a boredom so painful that it turned my stomach sour. I would lie in our hut alone, resenting my predicament, and when my companions came back I would walk across the parade grounds to get away from them. It was on one of these walks that I met the story-teller.

At first, when I saw the crowd gather around him, I walked away. I knew these story-tellers. Although my companions read nothing except the orders pinned on the regimental notice board, they would listen in complete silence to the story-tellers who moved around the encampment reciting sagas of lengthy inanity. This latest tale was likely to be as inane as the rest. But for some reason I stopped and listened to it, perhaps because even its inanity might provide some relief from my own tedium.

"It was when we serving in the tropics," said the story-teller. "It was as a result of a battery skin inspection that I lost them. Every week during the wet season they would line the battery up and the men would strip off and form up naked, in threes, so that the M.O. could see who had sweat blisters, who had tinea, who had ringworms, and anything else about our bodies that was not uniform. I was at the end of the line and the M.O. spent a long time looking at me. I had to look straight to my front while he looked down at them so I said for a joke: 'Do I get a blue ribbon, sir?' The M.O. told me not to be facetious, and had another look at them. Finally he turned to the medical orderly and said: 'He needs adjustment and re-alignment.' The orderly noted it down and they went off talking together. I heard someone laugh in the centre rank. I asked him what was so funny. Later on, after the parade was broken off the medical orderly came up and said: 'Soldier, you have to report to the M.O. Tuesday next so that you can get those adjusted and re-aligned.' 'Is that an order?' I asked. 'Yes,' he said. 'OK,' I said. I turned up at the medical centre on time. There was just the M.O. and the orderly. Everything seemed to be OK for a while, then suddenly the M.O. gave a grunt. I saw in the mirror that by accident he had almost cut them off. He searched in his instrument tray, but could not find what he was looking for. While he was looking for it they fell to the ground. 'That's a nuisance,' he said, and he picked them up and put them on the table. He talked for a while to the orderly and then he said to me: 'Look, soldier, I didn't know this was going to happen. Come back to-morrow. I won't be so busy then. Here,' he said as he gave them to me. 'Wrap them up in a bit of paper and put them in your pocket. Bring them along with you tomorrow at fourteen-thirty hours. That's all. Break off!' I came back the next day, a bit worried, but I didn't like to make too much fuss about it. The M.O. wasn't there. The orderly was filling in his returns. 'There's nothing I can do,' he said. 'It's a matter for the M.O., not me. I can't do anything about it.' 'When will he be back?' I asked. 'I don't know,' he said. 'Well, shit,' I said, 'can't you do anything about it?' 'No,' he said. 'Couldn't you tell the M.O. about it?' I said. 'He's been getting on to me a lot lately,' the orderly said. 'There are too many complaints and he blames me. Be a sport, will you, and don't say anything about it for a couple of days. You'll get me in the shit.' 'OK, sport,' I said. 'I'll come back some other time.' I told some of the other fellows about it, but most of them just laughed and said: 'The Army's like that.' But one of them said: 'Why don't you get paraded before the Battery Commander?' I didn't like worrying the officers, but I decided I'd better see the Battery Commander. He might do something. He listened to everything I had to say, then he said there was nothing much he could do. I asked him if he could see the M.O. He said, well, he couldn't do that, he wasn't supposed to interfere in medical matters. He thought I'd better go back to the medical orderly. I couldn't think of anything else to do, so the next day I went back to the medical centre. There was a new orderly. The other one had just been promoted and had gone away. The new orderly said the records were in a bloody awful mess, but he'd have a look for me in the files. He couldn't find anything, so he said he didn't think there was much he could do. But he asked me if he could have a look at them anyway. I emptied my pockets, but I couldn't find them. I said I thought I'd lost them. 'OK, that's all right then,' said the new orderly, 'I won't have to worry about it now.' I went back to my tent and looked through all my kit, but they weren't there. I had a look in the grass at the back of the tent, on the parade ground, in the back of the truck, in the mess hut, and in the Battery Commander's tent, but I still couldn't find them. I went to the Sergeant-Major and asked him if he had seen them. 'Were they wrapped up in a bit of paper?' he said. 'Yes,' I said. 'Well, soldier,' he said. 'I made an inspection of kit layouts this morning and I found them on your bed. They looked untidy and spoilt the appearance of the tent. The Battery Commander was going to make an inspection, so I threw them out.' 'That settles it,' I said. 'No, it doesn't,' he said. 'You'll have to do a week's defaulters for leaving rubbish hanging around your tent.' "

Most of the story-teller's audience did not see the point of his fable. To most of them the Medical Officer was the principal comedian of the story; they believed his castration of the central character was deliberate. I left them arguing about this and followed the story-teller across the parade ground. My boredom made me want to gain his respect. I asked him whether he had known that my companions did not understand what he was trying to tell them. Yes, he

33

said, he knew that. His grey eyes looked at me very straight. He was upright and square-shouldered and his lips were set in a way that was both self-mocking and bold. "I invented this tale some time ago. I thought they might become so enraged that they would do me some of the harm I deserved. They didn't. It's their favourite story. They don't understand it, but I keep on telling it as a way of reminding myself of the usual fate of an entertainer." I wanted to make him recognise my difference from the others. Perhaps he could help me. I was cunning enough, however, not to speak of my boredom; I tried to interest him by moralising about the expeditions. Speaking quickly but coolly he said: "Perhaps what disgusts you most is not some matter of general principle but the fact that you have nothing interesting to do." His grey eyes contemplated me. "For all I know you would be happier with an important and intelligent part in a bad cause than a boring and humble part in a good one." He walked away, still upright and square-shouldered, one leg slightly trailing.

Among some of the officers I had gained a reputation for malevolent stubbornness. Several days after seeing the story-teller—I was looking for him at the time, hoping to enjoy some more of his conversation—one of the officers, a small perky man like a grasshopper, called out to me to report to him at once. I ran over to him and stood there at attention for half an hour or so while he nibbled at me, saying that I had the brains of a general yet behaved like a malingerer. I stood silent and hot in the sun, summoning patience by delighting in the delicate tickle of the flies' feet touching off the nerves in my cheeks and forehead. The officer asked me if I realised that men such as my companions would have no purpose in life if there were no causes they could serve. I refused to comment. He sent me to the guardrooms to be punished.

I had learned something of the bestialities of the guardrooms, but as I heard the door shut me in, my first

34

impression of the guards was of such exaggerated malice that they seemed comedians made up as villains. Even after a fist hit my skull and two of them held me while the others interrogated me, I had this impression of a comic staginess. A huge-chested brute whose singlet flapped over the trousers of his uniform flexed his bullock arms so menacingly and frowned at me with such challenging simplicity that he seemed an actor overplaying a part. The others seemed equally over-theatrical — the two in the back row, their heads shaven, cigars sticking out of their mouths; the brooding, handsome youth, stripped to the waist, stroking his breasts; the bit players, glowering, scratching and spitting; the fat man with the wet face who stared at me, rubbing his hands together; the shyster in full uniform and neat glasses who with the pose of probity tricked me with his questions.

When they had finished and allowed me to dress again —their humiliation was finally so successful that I am not yet ready to describe it—they at once let me into their companionship by ignoring me with the same impartiality as they ignored each other except at some moment of wit. They began to look at some photographs, passing them from hand to hand with such anxious smiles that I assumed they were pornographic. I took one. It showed seven corpses dangling from a scaffold, all dressed in neat suits, their heads gravely inclined to one side, as if between them they were wisely considering some ponderous question. In another picture the naked corpse of a handsome and finely shaped young man sprawled, as in delight, on a chute, slipping towards a mass of other naked corpses. Another picture was of a starving little girl who looked trustingly at the camera with dark brown eyes; her hands clasped her legs with the innocent appeal of childhood, but her legs were shinbones sheathed in parched skin. They took this photograph from me and held it up so that they could all see it and laugh.

When I handed the rest of the photographs back to them without saying anything they hit me again. For the next few days they would lock me up, then let me out of my cage and hit me, then attempt to befriend me. When I failed to laugh at their jokes—all of them concerned with torture and murder—they would hit me again and put me back in my cage. They kept me caged in the guardroom itself, and even when I was locked up they might throw something at me or threaten me with the tortures that they said were carried out by specialists in some of the other guardrooms. But they seemed to want to recruit me as one of them.

Sitting in the cage, I yearned for their friendship, even for the companionship of the large brute with the shaven head and little ears who was their principal jester. I would try to joke with them when they hit me or laughed at me. As I began to know them better I saw that some of them would hold back from hitting; they would laugh as much as the rest when I was hit, but there was some restraint about them. With cunning, I decided to accept their offer and become a guard. I would, of course, be one of the moderate guards. Looking at them from my cage, I imagined how easy it would be to pretend to be like them. I could go on reminding myself that I was different, and later I could transfer to some other work in the encampments and be rid of them. Nobody would be harmed.

Then I remembered that although they laughed at their own jokes, they did not laugh at mine. Perhaps what was so tedious about them was that they were clowns and nothing else. Only their sense of fun impelled them, and it was an alien one. When I imagined myself as a guard a sense of great boredom seized me, more painful than the pain and humiliation of my life in the cage. And yet it would be so sensible to pretend to be like them, and by this means escape from them.

I was still wondering what I would do, when some

orders came. The guards unlocked the cage and, with a laugh and a few last kicks, let me out.

When I rejoined my companions in the encampment I felt ashamed of my whole person. It was as if, since it had been passed around by the guards, it was no longer fit to show to anyone else until it was clean again. There was a programme of drill going on and for some days I stamped my boots on the parade ground, trying to stamp out recollection of my doubts in the cage. My body ached and sweated, my thoughts jumbled into prickles of fatigue. It was a week or two before my principal emotion changed from shame back to boredom.

At about this time I again saw the story-teller. He was crossing between two huts and I ran after him to tell him of my disgust at the clownishness of the guards. He listened with what seemed a gentle sympathy, but when he replied he spoke coldly. "However tedious you found the conduct of the guards," he said, "was no compassion to be found for them? Can you love humanity but not know its atrociousness? Aren't the guards merely children? What is more like the amusing act of a child than hacking off a head?" His eyes turned away from me. "When we speak of the human species, don't we speak primarily of little children?" He walked away.

The next time I met him was at a special display in a distant encampment. When we arrived at the oval where the display was being held we advanced on it, tugging at our trousers, tightening our waistbands, pulling down our hats with those automatic movements with which soldiers approach any new event—as if it were a parade and they must smarten up for it. We had no interest in what we had come to watch. Flags flew from long poles, officers moved briskly across the oval, bands played. We slackened our belts, scratched ourselves, felt the sweat in our armpits, moved in our seats. We were all arms and boots. I went to the canteen, but there was no alcohol, so I bought soft drink. I pulled at the hairs on my hand. For some time I looked at the sunlight on my boots.

Then the story-teller sat down beside me. He was in a uniform different from the many I had already seen in the encampment. He said he had a staff car outside. Where would I like to go? I said that I wanted to know what kind of men gave orders to the encampments, sending us so meaninglessly here and there. "Some of the most talented men you could imagine," he said, leading me to the car. As it moved off he smiled at me, touched my arm, and said he would talk about murder.

His hands clasped on his lap, he spoke like a catechist who expected me to give a set answer; but he did not pause for it. "Except to those of the living who are inconvenienced by the death of others, where is the penalty of death? If death means oblivion, it means the end of suffering; if death means a radiant eternity it is a reward. In either case should we not laugh at it? Man must die. To organise his slaughter is revolting to the common membership of our species. But where is the pain for the slaughtered? Which of us could say that he would be better or happier by living a little longer?"

I replied that perhaps murder could be most effectively condemned as an act of dishonour to our species. The story-teller waved his hand at me, signalling me to go on. I said that our species might attain certain common assumptions which could make possible a kind of pride in ourselves, which could free us for action. At my mention of "pride" and "free" the story-teller showed a sort of shock, as if I had unexpectedly revealed a secret. He again signalled me to go on. I remained silent. He insisted, asking me what I meant and then explaining that the idea of "pride and freedom" might have more significance than I had intended. My use of it could perhaps later bring me to the attention of a very great personage.

"Yet," he said, "is there really any love of being

human?" He had adopted his catechist's manner again, and I did not reply. "In all the laughter and boasting you have heard about disaster, what mention has there been of humanity except in the specious sense that true humanity is seen embodied only in one special class of persons?" He repeated the phrase "pride and freedom" several times like a password. "Perhaps," he said, "it is all charades. Men act, then we all guess at the meaning. You spoke of a universal pride in our humanity. But murder is part of our humanity. Must we not then love murder too?"

He questioned me again and then advised me to go to sleep. When I woke up the car was parked beside a grey concrete building. The story-teller and his driver were gone.

Although itself of great size, the building was merely part of a complex of other brutish buildings, the whole so large that it seemed to serve some important purpose, since so much trouble could hardly have been taken for no reason at all. When the driver came back he said that it had been arranged for me to join one of the "planning halls" which directed one of the many enterprises of the encampments.

I found myself in a large conference room. Officials bustled around a table; messengers ran in and out. One of the officials hurried over to me. There was high excitement in him, but he spoke calmly. He was apologising to me because I was dressed in a uniform of low rank. He took me to a smaller room, waited outside while I changed into a uniform similar to his own, and then greeted me again, this time as if I were a friend.

There was some detachment and hesitancy about him. His young face was kept controlled, slightly frowning, but in his speech I felt now and again the high hope of one engaged on a great adventure. He led me into a room where we were joined by other officials, equally scholarly and softly spoken. At first I did not know what they were talking about, but gradually I learned that they were conducting an experiment connected with train movements. It was this that the bustle in the conference room was about, but they explained that this particular bustle was of a low order of importance. They would now take me to the centre of their activities.

I was in an enclosed space larger than the central hall of a major railway station, and as crowded. The roof, five or six stories high, was glassed over, and along the walls were elevated steel walks where officials hurried to adjust illuminated maps stretched from floor to roof; indicators several stories high flashed a variety of statistical information. Standards and flags in red, white and black were everywhere; military music was playing. Throughout the length of the floor was a vast relief map, with what looked like real water in its rivers and real snow on its mountains. On this lights flashed, indicating the movement of trains. From steel observation posts up on the wall, observers watched the detail of these movements with field glasses.

The band music stopped. An orator's voice screeched through the amplifiers. Everyone stood to attention and everything was still, except for the flashing of the lights on the maps and the clicking of the indicators. When the orator finished, a special cheer went up, repeated three times.

In the next few days, as I mastered the tasks they gave me, I did not know whether I was engaged in some huge and elaborate game or whether I was serving some significant purpose, but it seemed obvious that some of the complexities of the undertaking might become so absorbing that I would not care whether they served any purpose or not. Solving puzzles in planning halls seemed more diverting than doing foot drill in the encampments.

Except for those who enjoyed nothing but bustle itself, the excitement that impelled most of my new companions seemed more fear than hope. There was a general fear of the guardrooms that were embedded in the basement of the

40

building, and there was also a more diffuse kind of fear. Few of the individual plans succeeded in exactly the way they had been planned, and if it had not been that many of the other plans succeeded in spite of the planning the whole enterprise might have been an assembly mourning the necessity of disaster. However, despite individual senses of failure, an elation of success sustained the whole planning hall. It was as if an overall success had been built out of a series of particular mistakes.

At the beginning of my new work I spent most of the time at "briefings". On my first day I met a very senior official who, instead of talking to me, led me into a projection room; while someone switched on a slide projector and a tape-recorder he walked out again, and did not come back until the performance was over. On another occasion I sat in front of a man who held charts in front of me with the blazing eyes of one attesting to his faith while he recited what I could already read on the charts. As I met other officials it began to occur to me that it might be better if we simply exchanged pamphlets, charts, and coloured slides without talking to each other.

At the "major briefing", which was clearer than any of the earlier briefings, I sat among a hundred or so others and at last learned the details of the game played in the planning hall, in which I was now occupying a minor part in a subdivision of the Department of Commodity Processing. The greatest interest in this game lay in the number of variables. The "commodity" itself was unpredictable in certain ways, and so were supplies of fuel, labour, trains, and a great number of other things, including the weather. Above all it was in the chops and changes of grand policy that a great part of the excitement lay. We were told that one of our main objectives was to work out for each combination of variables when it arose the quickest method of assembling the "commodities" and transporting them to the processing plants. There were some millions of individ-

41

ual units of the "commodity". Given the great number of things that could go wrong, it was surprising that many of the "commodities" reached the processing plants.

In the second half of the presentation we were shown the warehouses where the by-products of the "commodities" were stored before distribution. We saw the piled bones of the corpses that had been burnt in the incinerators, the boxes of gold fillings taken from their teeth, the sacks of hair cut off before incineration, the clothes of the dead, sorted into sizes, the shelves of dolls and other playthings taken from children before they were gassed and burnt.

It was not so much a sense of horror as of tedium that made me get up and leave the briefing when I learned that the "commodities" were human beings. Out in the concrete corridor, I wondered at the inanity of so much of the more organised and intelligent activities of our species. The matter went from my mind, however, when a messenger summoned me to an interview with a dignitary of such importance that the whole enterprise in the planning hall, even though it appeared to dispose of millions of human lives, was to him only a matter of distant and minor interest.

The marshal's suite was on a high floor in a faraway building. I was told to wait in a large audience chamber where a conference had just ended. On the tables were ashtrays filled with cigar butts, half-eaten sandwiches, unfinished cups of coffee, crumpled documents, papers with lists of people's names on them, with ticks or crosses against them; in the darkness I could hear doors slam and men laugh. A liveried footman brought in brandy and fresh sandwiches.

I was looking through a window at other grey buildings when the marshal came in, shook my hand abruptly, gave an order to the footman, and hurried out. The footman brought in a uniform more splendid than the one I was wearing, explaining that the marshal had refused to give me an audience in my present uniform. When I was dressed in the new uniform the marshal came in again, at once sending away the sandwiches and brandy and ordering coffee and cream cakes. He complimented me on my powerful friends, saying that he had received orders to send me to the man they called "the martyr".

Despite his fatness he moved around in a lively way as he showed me some of his art treasures, all of which he had stolen; when he asked my opinion of them the stare of his pale blue eyes was attractively direct and his open laugh offered friendship. He leant back in an easy chair, his fat cheeks glistening and his medals gleaming, and told me boastful anecdotes of his inventiveness as an organiser. Waving a plump white hand, he gave instance after instance of how he had tossed random ideas among his men, muddling their plans and setting them running. Organisation to him seemed to be mainly an exciting jest, in which he would send men this way or that by flashes of his wit. His conversation was in disorder, but it shot out with such thrust that it set up around him the very presence of power in all its playful fancifulness. Even his cynicism gave him a kind of intellectual distinction, at least in these surroundings. In the guardroom it may not have been so distinctive.

When I questioned him about his connection with the operations in the planning hall he offered me a chocolate and explained that this was really the enterprise of some of his colleagues, although he knew something of it. He asked questions about what I had seen, excitedly making a note when I mentioned some example of incompetence. Then he leant forward, all honesty, his hands on his knees. Perhaps it did not matter all that much, he said; the "commodities" disposed of in the processing plants were scarcely human, were they? He leant back in his chair, one arm akimbo. It was true, he said, that he would not carry out such a programme if he were in direct control of such matters, at least not a programme of such proportions; for one thing it was a waste of resources—the traffic on the railways alone impeded many other great designs—and besides he himself did not usually kill humans for sport: for that purpose he killed animals.

He showed me photographs of some of the animals he had killed. Forgetting his earlier disclaimer, he told me more anecdotes of brutality, miming them out like a clown making laughter from misfortune. The first was of the beleagured city of an enemy where, while the guns crackled on its outskirts, humans dropped dead on the pavements from starvation, their bodies lying in their clothes as if they had taken a nap, until the authorities took them to the burial grounds where a million carcasses soon lay. Then he told me of a street the morning after a massacre, with the early rain gone, and the blood washed off, and sliced corpses still lying on the road. He recalled a distant camp lost in the snow, its prisoners struggling in rags along an icy road as inconsequentially as mist. He showed me a photograph of naked women pressed together in a queue, two of them holding naked babies in their arms. He admired the big breasts of one of them, and the buttocks of another, laughing and fingering the photograph as he prodded me with it. "I wouldn't really want to kill them," he said. "I'd sooner fuck them."

He was at the window when I began to question him about his frivolity. It was dusk but no lights had come on in the room. Outside it was raining. The grey light dulled his face and the shadows hollowed his cheeks so that he seemed old, haggard-eyed, condemned, although in fact he was merely bored. He listened to me flatly, saying nothing. Then he yawned and called to the footman to take me to "the martyr", adding derisorily that I seemed a fit companion for him. As I left, the lights went on and the fire was lit. His cheeks were again fat and pink; his medals sparkled; he was reaching for a telephone and calling for a glass of champagne.

44

It was dawn when we reached the apartments of "the martyr". The lights were still on, and I was told to wait until a conference had finished. Through the windows, I watched the greyness of the dawn become the greyness of the buildings. It was raining again. I thought for a while of the dawn when we had landed on the beach where I was to die. Behind me there was a movement of men leaving the apartment. The lights went off. It was now very quiet. Someone said that the martyr would see me now. I walked through two rooms into the conference chamber. The long table was empty, except for its litter of paper, but at one of the big windows someone was looking at the rain. The door closed. We were alone.

He came towards me with a slight limp. His eyes looked steadily enough into mine, but there was a trace of apology in a sudden gesture of his hand as the man I had thought of as the story-teller told me that he had hoped to call me soon, but that he was somewhat inconvenienced by my arriving so unexpectedly. He asked me to come to the window with him and watch a procession.

The buildings in the square seemed the colour of grey sand, clotted in smoke, and damp with dirty rain. Slogans hovered limply from moored balloons. In the square's centre was a small grubby park. Pale light fell on the grime of the leaves and the patches of bare earth among the trodden grass. To one side there was a statue in grey stone of an orator in a frock coat, one arm upstretched. Most of the crowd were in black overcoats.

Troops flooded down the street, bearing their arms like refuse on a flooded river. When the siege guns and rockets rolled through the square they threatened the sky with their shininess. From a balcony in one of the buildings across the square a leader watched the procession, almost wistfully, as if there were something he had forgotten to do and would now never remember. But once he began speaking, and the crowd roared, his tongue flapped

45

like a maniac's and his face was contorted with such ecstasy that he might have been in simultaneous coition with every one of them.

When the crowd had gone and the noise was coming from another part of the city, the story-teller said: "You have seen an army that will never fight anybody. It is the same, of course, in all the planning halls and with all the expeditions. Every action in which you participated there was senseless. There couldn't be any result to it. How could there be, when there can be no more deaths?

"It was once hoped here—long ago, in one of the reform movements—that allowing these re-enactments might finally convince them of their folly. Instead they set about elaborating their old activities, although there could no longer be any result to them. Apparently they are prepared to go on with fakeries for ever. The contrivances of their leaders in creating false senses of danger were beyond even our imagination—although, as ever, we can't know how much they believe and how much they deliberately contrive."

There was a roar from the distant crowd. "Is this what you mean when in the pride of belief you find freedom of action?" said the story-teller. Even more coldly, and for the first time as if there was no fault in himself, he said: "Mightn't it be that the principal achievement of greatness is to add self-importance to wickedness? Perhaps the final function of a great idea is to dignify base actions with a little decency."

He then returned to a style of self-derision, telling me of the circumstances of his martyrdom with such confidently modest and tentative allusiveness that out of politeness I made gestures to indicate that such a famous man need not introduce himself to me. He explained, however, that he spent so much of his time in the encampments and among the enterprises of the complex of grey buildings because it provided a form of self-mortification for the results of his earlier actions.

At the time when he had been contemplating the possibility of martyrdom he was aware of his ambitions, so that at first he had regarded it as a temptation he must resist. Then he had decided that he must sacrifice himself to his pride. He had believed that the immediate result of his defiance would be the massacre of his followers and that in this there might be salvation for *them,* or at least glory; to immolate himself and so many others would be to set alive an ideal that might finally testify to faith. "Perhaps," he said, "the way you might put it was that I was concerned with setting a good example. After such an act there was for me no possibility of reward. I now punish myself by seeking the company of heroes and by debasing myself in their acts." He then reminded himself that the irony of his martyrdom was that his followers had not gained salvation by following him to the flames: they had recanted, thereby glorifying his own bravery, if that was the word for it, although damning themselves.

He led me to a room where I could sleep while he got on with his affairs. As he was leaving I said that I had thought of him as "the story-teller", but now I knew that he was called "the martyr". He cut in, saying that my description of him might be more accurate than history's, since the principal function of martyrdom was to provide us with stories that might illuminate our belief in our species. But despite his sharpness I felt myself at last in the presence of a noble and triumphant intelligence, benign in intention and magnanimous in enterprise.

The pavement was cold as we walked down a shabby little lane between two of the grey buildings. It was night and the story-teller was taking me to dinner. "You have seen something of the worst side of heroism," he said. "I have now gathered together for dinner a better class of hero so that you might get some idea of the best that can be expected from this type of person."

47

The inside of the restaurant glittered with lacquer and mother-of-pearl. As I sat down with the heroes the story-teller had gathered together, a confusion of dishes—two dozen or more—were quickly placed on the table. We nibbled at this and that. Bottles were flourished, and most of the dishes were left untouched. One of the girls, perky and gossipy, was giving cheek to the chairman of this table of heroes; another kept trying to tempt us to eat some of the thinly sliced bits and pieces, offering them to us on toothpicks.

The heroes spoke of their failures. One of them told me how, in the recklessness with which he had served a cause in his youth, he was praised for his integrity. But when, to do good, he accepted power among his enemies, he was reviled. Children were still taught the hateful meaning of his name. A tall, handsome hero tapped my knee: he told me of the boredom of a high office he had held, which he maintained simply for the harm he could prevent, and the sake of his family. When he was dismissed he was stripped of his wealth. His family and his cause suffered, but he himself was happy. After his death his name became that of a hero who had sacrificed power for principle, yet it was among the trivialities and disappointments of office that his suffering had occurred.

"Perhaps it is only fame that political leaders can sensibly take into account," said the story-teller, lighting a cigar. "All other matters over which politicians must show concern can be so contingent and accidental that, while doing the best one can in the meantime, true political genius may lie in knowing how to wait for chance to fashion out of events some memorable and exemplary drama." The smoke of his cigar wandered over the uneaten food.

Hands reached out. Each of the heroes piled food onto the three or four plates in front of him. They ate with the interest of those who have just started a meal. Then they began to gossip, one or other of them breaking off now and then to flirt with the girls. I tried to talk to the girl beside me. She gave me a decent minimum of courtesy, but when I began listening to the heroes she was content with my inattention and sat gazing across the room with a faint smile. All the conversation now was about someone called "the Prince", and I understood nothing of it. Did the Prince merely use his followers for some temporary purpose, and then abandon them? This seemed their main concern. But then they also spoke affectionately of the Prince's cunning and audacity. One of them referred to him as "the greatest of us all". Then I heard more complaints against the Prince's habit of betrayal, combined with an apparently contradictory confidence that his old comrades would nevertheless rally to his new cause.

After the others had gone I sat for a while with the story-teller. He told me that he had arranged for me to travel across a lake to meet a friend of his—or a kind of friend (there was no certainty in his friendship, or in anything else about him) who had concerned himself with the speculative side of man's nature. I would know him by the name of "the illusionist". He explained that the Prince himself had heard of me and was anxious that, since I had seen something of men of action I should go on to see something of men of contemplation.

"The special interest the Prince has shown in you comes from your use of the words 'pride and freedom'," said the story-teller. "These words are part of the rhetoric the Prince is now assembling for his coming revolt. That is why I was so interested when you used them—and why I put your use of them on record."

He gestured that there were to be no questions, but when I asked who the Prince was he replied, as if politely but uninterestedly giving a stranger a street address, that the Prince was the personage, or idea, or whatever it was, that I would probably think of as Lucifer, or Satan.

CHAPTER 5

the third adventure

I met the illusionist beside the lake. He was sitting on a black rock watching me as if he were as much part of me as I was part of the lake, his body as still as the rock and his eyes and hair as black. His arm flicked towards me like a knife, then froze until, withered by the theatricality of its gesture, it dropped. He walked round behind me, so that I could not see him when he began to talk, although I could feel the bone of his hands on my back.

He described the lake as I saw it, and then, with his words, he seemed to destroy the lake; it was still there, but it was there in some other way—a space, without shape or colour or weight, in which there were chance occurrences that were unimaginable; all that there seemed to existence was a turbulence of nothingness.

When my own sense of the lake reappeared he was sitting beside me on the grass, again describing the lake as I had seen it. I could feel the tautness of his legs and the tightness of his laugh. "It is my best trick," he said. "Perhaps the only one that works. With the words I use I seem to be able to give the illusion of a denial of sensation itself. I was, of course, simply saying that the impressions *you* get of the lake—its apparent colour and shape, its wetness, its weight, and so forth—are not *really* the lake; they are simply shadows of the body's conventions and limitations, recordings of the particular sensations which we conveniently mistake for existence. How can we do otherwise? They are our only connection with it."

He got up, stretched his legs, and motioned me up. "We can talk as we go to the wharf," he said. "You are going on a journey." We passed on to a sandy path, and into the glumness of a pine forest. "What we see in the lake is illusion," he said, "but it might be equally illusory to imagine that the lake is *really* nothing but space and nuclear and molecular activity; it might be other things as well, beyond our guessing; it seems likely that the lake is not *really* any particular thing. It would depend simply —if I might be platitudinous—on one's point of view." He paused, and then took off what I now saw to be his black wig and put on a blond one; he changed his false eyelashes correspondingly and the glass discs he wore inside his eyesockets, over his eyeballs. He said nothing more, but mumbled to himself a little and made a gesture or two, as if rehearsing his next role.

We came out on another part of the lake, where there were several wharves, with a ferry moored to one of them. "Now you must go to the conference," he said. "The ferry leaves soon. They'll tell you about it on the way, but it's intended . . ." He broke off, gesturing slightly and smiling. "It is *intended* to settle some of the problems of what part intellectuals can play in the world of affairs." He looked at me, as if expecting me to laugh, then busied himself with handing me tickets and several files of documents. Just before I got on the ferry he put a hand on my arm. "The construction of the illusion that there is a system in events is the intellect's highest power," he said. "How can we do anything if we don't know or care whether things are one way or the other? To act we must be transfixed by some pattern. Philosophy? Religion? Poetry? Science?

51

Rhetoric?" His voice dropped with each question, and he seemed to be speaking to himself, without interest. "Yet, although the intellect consoles us, giving what I call freedom through faith, and what you and the Prince, in a somewhat different context, would call freedom through pride, how can the patterns it makes be *true*?" As he walked away he plucked off his eyelashes and pulled the discs off his eyes.

At first the ferry was empty, but it quickly filled. It swung slowly in an arc, turning from the wharf towards the water of the horizon. It stirred and quivered, lifted itself almost out of the water, and shot across the lake, cutting it into ribbons of blue and white. At the buffet lunch I sat beside a woman with whom I spent the rest of the journey. From her I learned that the conference we were to attend had been arranged by the governments of two rival islands, Blue Island and Mauve Island, that lay far out across the lake.

She had about her the beginning of ripeness, and also a certain boyishness: she seemed to show both wisdom and bodily liveliness. As I listened with keenness to her description of the two islands they became her two breasts, set on the firm surface of her skin, and as she spoke of the views that separated the intellectuals of the two islands these views became her two thighs, held upright and separate.

The people of the two islands, she said, lay under the threat of a larger power on a nearby shore of the lake. The guns of their two small armies pointed at the shore, not at each other. There were other matters on which they co-operated, such as the ferry services that ran between them, replacing a bridge that had been blown up by saboteurs from their joint enemy; but so much ingenuity went into trying to build the sentiment that each island was totally different from the other that their most useful mutual relationship was their quarrelling, which stimulated each of them to a greater sense of purpose. They had

52

argued so vindictively about where the conference was to be held that agreement was reached only when they decided to anchor a boat midway between the two islands and hold the conference there. Although the people of both islands came from the same race (as did their enemy on the shore), they claimed entirely different histories; although both islands were equally prosperous, Blue Island saw itself as rich and Mauve Island as poor; although their systems of government were similar, Mauve Island professed the pragmatic style and Blue Island the heroic; and although their climate was the same, Blue Island saw itself as hot and Mauve Island as cold. The rebels in both islands were in gaol.

I imagined the woman's flesh: its wetness and dryness, its tightness and slackness, its softness and firmness; and when we landed on Blue Island (where half of us were to stay while the other half were to stay on Mauve Island) I scarcely noticed our hosts; throughout the long dinner held in our honour I spoke only to her. We were sitting alone on a balcony in our hotel when I touched her hand. She stood up, smiling. In the moonlight her shaven skull gleamed like a gravestone; her hair lay on the floor; her gums grinned. The illusionist moved over to a dark corner of the balcony, near his bedroom. He apologised for deceiving me and went into the bedroom, leaving me alone.

As we drove past the security guards and through the lawns and trees towards the mansion where the leader of Blue Island was to entertain us at lunch, I was as concerned as the others at the prospect of meeting him. Throughout the morning's drive in the city that made up most of the island, its motor-cars bumper to bumper in the prosperous parts, the streets bustling even in the poorer quarters, the talk had been all of the leader and his control of what its people saw as their important and progressive nation. His opponents were scattered and disarrayed by his brilliance of manoeuvre; his supporters quoted with enthusiasm instances of his sarcasm, his drive for domination, and even the gossip about his habits of ruthlessness.

Inside the mansion was a large reception room, all white and silver. I looked out through its windows, misty because of the air-conditioning, over a terrace of gleaming red tiles and a sweep of green lawn to a cluster of flowering trees. Aloof until now, smiling but silent, the leader began his speech of welcome. He teased us with his wit. There was no arrogance about it—his speech was delivered with such shyness and diffidence that later some of his guests said he was merely an ordinary man trying to make his visitors feel at home—but there were stings and barbs, and prickling allusions to many of the guests (in particular those from his own city). Although he mentioned most of those present, referring in pauses to a list, my name did not come up; but like the others I listened for some mention of myself. We were like schoolchildren waiting for their end-of-term reports. For lunch we sat at long tables and talked of the brilliance of the leader, shivering in the cold—even the food was iced—and wondering if he might come and speak to us.

In the car on our way to the next reception, two of my companions, delighted by his references to them, praised his brilliance. The other two, stung by his wit, complained of his unfairness.

The mansion where the leader of Mauve Island received us for dinner was made up of small rooms, cosy with wooden panelling, with an open fire in each of them. In the largest, young people slowly revolved in the folk dances of the island. For hours waiters brought us small steaming dishes of food which we were to eat where we stood, exhausted by the heat and the noise of the music. The leader of Mauve Island walked among us as if he were a visitor in his own house. We heard anecdotes of the great shrewdness of his long silences, the meticulous selectiveness of his apparent indifference. When I met him his hot, tired eyes showed nothing but their tiredness and the slackness of his lips his boredom. Speaking very softly, he told me about his children.

Although they had spent only a day in the two islands, the intellectuals visiting the conference were now clearly divided into supporters of Blue Island and supporters of Mauve Island, and much of their conversation was concerned with the details of the disputes between the two. Those who considered themselves insulted by the leader of Blue Island praised the heat of the Mauve Island mansion, comparing it favourably with the coldness of the air-conditioning of the Blue Island mansion. Those who were offended by the silences of the leader of Mauve Island criticised the excess of his food. Some found the lunch over-spiced; some found the dinner insipid. Some spoke of the evident patriotism of the speech made by the leader of Blue Island, others of the evident patriotism of the folk dancers on Mauve Island. Just before we left I spoke again to the leader of Mauve Island; he told a long and wistful story about the leader of Blue Island: it went back to their days as students together, when they were friends.

Before the conference opened on the next day soldiers carrying landmine detectors searched the conference boat for explosives; armed security guards marched up and down its decks. There had been news that morning of riots in the main city of the nation that threatened both of the islands; one of the most important ministers in its government had been dismissed and its principal leader had made a vindictive speech accusing the governments of the two islands of sabotage.

Wearing academic gowns, and in an order determined by tossing a coin, the two leaders formally opened the conference. The green light in the room gave us all the appearance of lying inert in a fishbowl, either asleep or dead. Only the speakers were obviously alive, although sluggishly; they moved their lips as if sucking, and occasionally swished a hand as if changing direction. There was a banquet, and after this the first working session began.

We were seated at a hollow triangle made up of long, gleaming black tables. On the one side, rugged up against the cold, were the intellectuals from Mauve Island; on the other, in open-necked shirts because of the heat, were the intellectuals from Blue Island; the visitors sat at the base. Speaking ponderously, and moving his head slowly from side to side, a speaker from Blue Island tried to persuade us, at some length, that events must be thought of as a line. This so affronted the intellectuals from Mauve Island—who believed that events were not a line but a circle—that they at once threatened to withdraw from the conference. There was an adjournment, during which some of the visitors sitting at the base drafted a statement putting forward a compromise view that events were both a line and a circle and therefore might be thought of as a wave. The intellectuals from both islands attacked this view as insultingly typical of the insensitivity of the visitors, and the conference was saved only when all three sides agreed that a sub-committee would be set up to report on the geometry of existence. To ensure that this matter did not again disrupt the conference it was agreed that the sub-committee's report would not be prepared until after the conference was over.

The evening reception was on Blue Island. Most of the guests were drunk before it began, and the reception hall drummed with noise. The illusionist said little—the talk was mainly gossip about the islands—but in one of the hotel bedrooms later, he and a group of his friends, among spilt liquor and billowing tobacco smoke, all began to shout so loudly that there were complaints from other rooms. At breakfast next morning the illusionist said that it was useful to shout at one's friends because it allowed one to argue with oneself; one could then go away and think about it later.

When we arrived at the conference room that morning we found it turned into a rubbish tip—stones, plants, sticks, articles of clothing, cans, bottles, and several hundred other things. Attendants at one end of the heap were moving these pieces of rubbish around, putting them here and there, as if looking for some pattern in them; others, at the opposite end, were laying out each bit of rubbish separately and making notes. A lecturer standing on a box in the middle of the heap said that each piece of rubbish was an "observation" gathered by a "research worker". He assured us that this was the only true method of finding out what things were like, and explained that it would take a great deal of work to determine what conclusions all of these individual observations would add up to. We broke off early for lunch.

Most of the visitors were missing, having gone off to one or other of the islands to see the sights. To allow the rubbish to be cleared away there was to be a free afternoon, but just as we were setting off to enjoy it, the missing visitors returned; they had believed that there was to have been an afternoon session and that the morning session was free. When they saw the rubbish they went back to see more of the sights.

In the hotel after that evening's reception the illusionist and his friends again shouted at each other, although they now seemed to have changed sides. At breakfast the illusionist said drunken argument was simply a question of exercise and even if seizing advantage meant contradicting oneself, when recollected later this was a lesson in what it might have been like to be someone else.

There was a delay before we began the third day's session. A fundamental disagreement had come up between the delegates from the two islands, and there were rumours that the conference might close. The organising committee was holding a special meeting. The trouble had arisen because the delegates from Mauve Island had wished to issue a manifesto saying that intellectuals were essentially traditionalists upholding the best in the past, its goodness lying in its irrelevance to the present. This was in direct contradiction to a manifesto that the delegates from Blue Island were preparing; it said that intellectuals were essentially revolutionaries, upholding what seemed the best in the present, its goodness lying in its irrelevance to the future. Both sides were threatening to withdraw. The chairman of the organising committee had drafted another manifesto which suggested that intellectuals should not contaminate themselves by action, but that nevertheless by their wisdom they were the only persons qualified to judge action, so that they were uniquely experts in matters about which by definition they knew nothing. This led to a division between the chairman and the secretary, who, in a manifesto of his own, announced that the intellectual must act, but that he should do so with an idealism that would ensure that he would achieve nothing. The dispute was again settled by setting up a sub-committee which, this time, by amendment, was given instructions to make no report at all.

When at last the session began, one delegate stood on a table and farted as loudly as he could while other delegates danced to music played on hollow bamboo sticks. Another delegate then picked his nose while three others beat drums. Then four delegates took off their clothes and re-enacted a hunting scene painted on the wall of the tomb of an Egyptian nobleman. At this stage the delegate who had begun the proceedings by farting objected to the element of cultural imitativeness in this re-enactment whose artificialities, he maintained, defeated the whole purpose of the discussion, which was that of naturalness and spontaneity. Others attacked him for using words instead of merely expressing himself; even language was an artificial convention. One of them tried to stop him talking by kissing him on the mouth; another stood on a chair and pissed on him. When it was over, and lunch was ready, a visitor sang a song in which he said he had found the session a deeply moving experience, the only meaningful event in the whole conference, because of its removal from mere rationality to more basic and much deeper motivations. The man who had been pissed on went away and had a shower.

When we returned to the conference room in the afternoon we found it largely given over to charts and diagrams. Each of us was handed several thick dossiers of statistical tables, with apologies that other tables had not yet been duplicated but would be forwarded to us after the conference. An argument developed at once about the mathematics of one set of the tables. I whispered questions to one of the delegates and learned that the charts and diagrams had been prepared by a sect which believed that human conduct could be described only by what could be measured, which meant that it could scarcely be described at all. The argument about the mathematics of the disputed tables continued until the end of the session, and I did not learn what aspects of human conduct the charts and diagrams were believed to represent. No one complained about this omission.

In the next session another argument started when a delegate from Blue Island read a paper in which he maintained that the function of an egg was to produce another egg. He demonstrated this by a film on the life of a hen. This was followed by a paper by a delegate from Mauve Island maintaining that the real purpose of an egg was to add to the general display of existence. He demonstrated this with coloured reproductions of a number of works of art which showed the influence of human concepts of the egg. One of the visitors then argued that eggs had no purpose at all, nor did anything else. He did several conjuring tricks with eggs to support his point. The discussion was concluded by another visitor who, after describing himself as a humanist, spoke of the usefulness of the egg to our species. To support his hypothesis he gave a cooking demonstration.

In the hotel bedroom after that night's reception the illusionist was again shouted down by his friends. He gestured with contempt and walked out into the corridor. He was tired, and was beginning to take off his disguise, a sight so sad that I said good-night and walked away. But at breakfast the next morning he seemed cheerful enough. He remarked that perhaps one reason why some men wrote books or made speeches was that they could not win drunken arguments with their friends.

It was his turn to address the conference. He walked to the apex of the triangle of black tables, speaking so gently that to begin with he gained attention. Across the blue of the lake, tiny in its horizon, a saffron crash-boat was bouncing across the water. Like a great leader or a great thinker it was making its own turbulence.

"Shouldn't we first acknowledge how jumpy our brains are? How sticky our consciousness? How incomplete our senses?" The illusionist paused. Someone laughed. "And shouldn't we then recognise our stupefying obsessions? Our excitements in the brutal battles of controversy? Our ravenous appetites for fame? The corruption of our disciples? Or our self-pitying and nervous seeking of misfortune?"

The crash-boat was larger now. It seemed to be heading straight for our own boat. In their yellow mackintoshes and life-jackets, its crew stood up very still, like winged messengers bringing some grave warning.

"Most of those who scorn the practical are nevertheless not notably creative or critical," said the illusionist. "The more diligent of them are those whose minds are orderly enough for them to *learn off* the creations of others, which they can repeat word-perfect. They are not creative enough

60

to be practical." The crash-boat seemed only a minute or so away, still heading for us. Fear silenced everyone except the illusionist.

The crash-boat stopped. It flopped in the water as its crew threw lines aboard. There was something familiar about the uniforms under their mackintoshes, and even about the faces of two of them.

"Is it not possible," said the illusionist, "that everything stated at this conference about intellectuals could, with all its contradictions, nevertheless all be true?" The guards' feet were on the deck. Their leader was speaking to the captain. They came into the room and mounted sentries at the doors. The delegates were silent, but the illusionist was still talking, at the same time writing on a blackboard. "Let us imagine one kind of intellectual," he said. "We shall call him an intelligent-creative-ignorant-radical intellectual. We have all met him." The leader of the guards beckoned two other guards and they walked towards the illusionist. "Consider the subtle difference," said the illusionist, "between an intelligent-uncreative-ignorant-conservative intellectual and an *unintelligent*-uncreative-ignorant-conservative intellectual."

He stopped speaking. The crash-boat lay still outside. A guard opened one of the doors of our saloon, clicked his heels and stood beside it at attention. The illusionist and the guards officer were talking softly. One guard came behind the illusionist and seized his arms. Another stood behind my chair, his hands gripping my back. The illusionist was marched over to me. "They want us both," he said in a loud voice. "We are under arrest."

As soon as the crash-boat moved off, the illusionist began to change from one disguise to another, doing it piece by piece, seeming to merge from the semblance of a young man into that of an old man. When he had finished, and the "guards" had changed their uniforms for more ordinary

61

dress, he explained that our arrest was a carefully contrived *frisson* designed partly to remove him from the tediums of the conference and partly to provide its principal "happening". He said that although he despised such voguishness, his mission demanded that he should be familiar with fashions, and indeed, in a broad sense, it was only through fashion that our species could do anything. "As in many other matters," he said, "we must remain cheerful, despite this limitation on our freedom, for the very good reason that there is nothing else we can do about it."

He explained that his new disguise was that of an ageing academician and that he was taking me to a great building, called The Cloisters, where many of the people I had met at the conference had been trained. Water flashed around the crash-boat for several more hours. Eventually we reached a jetty. Women were digging in the grey mud for the tubers of lotus plants, piling them up and wrapping them in the soft flesh of their own leaves before putting them in boxes. The illusionist said that these tubers had once been considered a great delicacy at The Cloisters but were now out of vogue.

The whole plain ahead of us was taken up with buildings and gardens, each of them some reconstruction of the past. Behind them rose a huge tower of a building, erect with outrageous confidence, its glass sparkling in the sun, its concrete piercing the clouds. A great electric sign proclaimed it The Cloisters. Inside it, thousands of young people swarmed on escalators and in lifts and corridors. We were met by several of the officials of the place, who treated the illusionist with great respect, taking him off at once and leaving me waiting. After a while a girl of twenty or so came up and explained that she was my guide. She said that she would now show me some of the mysteries of this place.

She took me first into an ampitheatre where several thousand young people sat around an old man with the wild white hair and fixed gaze of a prophet; he was speaking to them through a microphone from a dais which slowly revolved so that they could all see his face in turn as they wrote down his words.

Explaining that this type of ceremony was now becoming démodée, my guide said she would show me two of the newer ceremonies, from which, until recently, much had been expected. She took me into another hall, as large as the first, where several thousand young people sat facing a white screen on which was projected a film of the same old white-haired man; they, too, were putting his words in their notebooks. We moved on to what seemed a large floor in a factory, where several thousand young people sat in silence with earphones on their heads. When I picked up one of the earphones I again heard the voice of the old white-haired man.

The girl and I had some coffee in the canteen. Without touching it or even looking at it, I could feel the shape of her body beside me and the slight movements of her breasts and belly, the crossings of her thighs. When I looked at her brown eyes, she looked back with a little smile, as if there was nothing she was not prepared to guide me in. I looked away. I had begun to suspect that she was simply the illusionist in yet another disguise.

After lunch she took me to a chamber where thousands of young people sat at tables and chairs, writing. She explained that they were being subjected to one of the periodical "trials"—tests of how much they could remember of what the old white-haired man had told them. The punishment for failure at these trials was expulsion. We moved into another testing chamber, where the officials of the building themselves faced the trials that determined their promotion. Some of their written reports were being put on scales and weighed. I was told that the official whose reports weighed the most would receive the next promotion.

At dinner we were lectured by an official who spoke to us of discipline and rigour and of the tidiness and obedience of the mind. Another official spoke of the tricks the young would sometimes get up to—pretending interest in matters that bored them when they were being tested—and the methods he was using to catch them out. Another spoke of the necessity of drudgery for its own sake, as if to work at anything, however trivial, was better than to be wise, or useful, or even merely idle. Another spoke of the need for officials to labour at their reports, as if The Cloisters were a dungheap that rose in esteem with its height and the purpose of the officials was to increase that height by the volume of their deposits on it.

It was nearly midnight. My guide touched my hand lightly and smiled. She was leading me down a corridor. I again thought of her thighs and breasts—and of the disguises of the illusionist. She led me into a big hall, tumultuous with noise. Young people sprawled all round it, shrieking. Shouts announced revolt. From microphones came screams for the seizure of The Cloisters and the expulsion of its officials. My guide leant towards me, her breast touching me. "The Cloisters is an institution of secret violence," she said. She leant more heavily against me. "We must make this violence show its face." There was a fresh shout. Someone shrieked for the burning of The Cloisters so that all could be free. In the confusion a resolution was passed. There were loud cheers.

I went with my guide to her room, still suspecting some trick. When she put my hand between her thighs my hesitation went, but when our business was over I suspected that perhaps the illusionist could produce even this deceit. I made references to our experiences on Mauve Island and Blue Island, believing that if this girl was merely one of the illusionist's disguises I might trick him into revealing himself. But the girl was asleep, or appeared to be. In my dreams I was back in the encampment; our officers were shouting at us to free The Cloisters, but it was not clear whether we were to free it of its officials or its young, or to free ourselves of both them and The Cloisters itself.

I had meant to wake before the girl, to test one of my theories as to her reality as a woman, but when I opened my eyes she was already reading. Passion again overcame suspicion, and when it was finished I again began to doubt. On our way to breakfast the girl gave me a quick smile that seemed exactly the same as the illusionist's.

In the cafeteria we drank coffee with one of the officials. I had promised the girl I would not speak of the young people's meeting of the night before, but the official seemed already to have received a full report on it. He assured me that a system of bulkheads had already been put into operation so that any area of disturbance could at once be shut off from the rest of the building.

As he said this a group of young people burst into the cafeteria, bearing black and red flags. They said the moment of liberation had come and we must all prepare to accept our freedom. After throwing tables and chairs into barricades across the doors, they held a meeting that lasted five hours. Manifestos went up on the walls, denunciations went through loud hailers. There were rumours that armed security guards would break through the barricades. There was said to be fighting in the corridors.

They stayed in possession of the cafeteria for six days. Sentries stood at the barricades all night. Committees formed and re-formed. Typewriters and duplicating machines produced pamphlets, leaflets, bulletins. There was continuous gossip about new developments, rumours about other revolts in the building, new steps in negotiation, new strategies and prospects. Slogans and obscenities were scrawled on the walls until there was no room left for more; this was attacked as censorship, and the walls were washed down several times in the interests of free expression, although some then claimed that this in turn was an act of censorship against those who had scrawled on the walls in

65

the first place. There was an almost permanent state of public meeting as the young people debated the purpose of their revolt in many resolutions and counter-resolutions. At the end of the six days the food had run out and it was time for some of the trials to be held. The barricades were dismantled; the young people went off to the testing chambers.

There was open libertinage during these six days and the girl and I took advantage of it, thrusting at each other whenever we wished before anyone who cared to watch. I still suspected at times that the body with which I shared this delight was really that of the illusionist, intricately disguised in some way I could not understand. My suspicions would go when the girl expressed an innocence I could not imagine the illusionist capable of simulating; then they would return when she let slip some remark suggestive of what I took to be a degree of understanding of our species that I would not have expected from the rest of the young rebels in the cafeteria. The matter was still unsettled when the siege ended and I said good-bye to her, having been called to one of the highest floors of the building.

I was now amongst officials who quoted drily from texts in a process that was not so much a conversation as an exchange of documents. They expressed a faith in the division of their labours that became so great that those who were devoted to one labour were incapable of talking or listening to any of the others.

Reports came up to us of occasional tumult below. The young people had seized a library for two days and burnt some of its books; when some of the girls bared their breasts to deride the white hair of the old man on the revolving dais he had declared that he would not speak into the microphone any more; the office of one of the officials had been invaded and the official held as hostage until security guards relieved him. When the young people began pissing on the guards from the windows the guards punched and kicked them, threw them down stairs, and clubbed them. The discussion over coffee of the young people's heroic action was intelligent and sympathetic; many theories were advanced to account for their conduct.

I was put to work for a while in one of the catalogue rooms. These rooms filled the greater part of the public space on the upper floors, and those who worked in them had a particularly intense feeling of purpose. Their aim, it was said, was to catalogue the whole body of knowledge and speculation. For convenience' sake, this was done in a number of different divisions, most of the members of which knew little or nothing of what was happening in other divisions. I was told that an attempt to bring all the divisions under one catalogue had failed and that this experiment was unlikely to be repeated. As I moved among the filing-cabinets of the subdivision to which I had been sent I soon discovered that some of them were almost empty, or quite empty, despite the classifications carefully printed on them; other cabinets were filled, but sometimes with cards so old as to be illegible. There were "waiting-rooms" in which thousands of cards lay unsorted. One day news came of developments in the subdivision of the division of knowledge with which we were concerned—developments which seemed to demand either the abolition of our subdivision or an entirely new system of classification. After a long meeting, it was decided that abolition of the subdivision was out of the question. We began devising new classifications to paste on the filing-cabinets. There was no suggestion that we could attempt a reclassification of the actual contents of the cabinets.

Around this time I saw the illusionist—in the disguise he had been wearing when I first met him. Following him, I found myself in a lecture theatre. He had already started speaking from the rostrum. Most of the seats in the theatre were empty, and those who were there seemed to show little interest in what the illusionist was saying. Some were talking softly; the rest looked stupid with mere politeness. Behind the rostrum a blackboard was covered with scrawls from an earlier lecture; a tap dripped into a sink set into the rostrum; the microphone whistled faintly. The illusionist had adopted a diffident, sincere manner, speaking directly to four or five people in the audience whom he seemed to have chosen as worthy of his attention.

He had begun by pointing out that the stock gesture of many artists and thinkers of the present age was one of contempt or despair, so that while some of the ordinary people had begun to enjoy the creature comforts which earlier generations could only imagine as part of an after-life, the age was now presented by many of its most sensitive thinkers as one of extraordinary unhappiness and confusion —in some cases, as an age that should be destroyed.

What most aroused these thinkers, he suggested, was that events in their own time did not seem to fit the pattern of existence as they had learned it in books. They projected the inadequacies of their own crisis of vision into a description of the world, by this means getting their own back on it. The illusionist paused. Either mistaking his intention, or politely pretending to do so, about half the small audience left.

"Humans need a new sense of tradition," he said, after waiting to see if any more wished to leave, "so that they can re-invent the past to make it more relevant to how they imagine the future. But they also need a new commonsense of their own sensations. They need a new if more sceptical kind of faith in the evidence of their own observations. To decide that the end points of existence are not hard bits and pieces but a mysterious activity that usually can be thought of as either a wave or a particle, as either energy or matter, may baffle the body's senses, but it could work wonders for the sense of humour of our species."

The microphone broke down, and the illusionist was forced to shout out the rest of his speech in a way that seemed to disconcert him; he made several false emphases and many false gestures. He spoke of the puzzle that most chemical reactions came from chance collisions of molecules which were nevertheless predictable. Why was this pattern predictable? To this, he said, there was no answer.

"A human," he said, "is no longer an absolute observer. He is part of his own experiment, part of his own observation. When matter dissolved into mathematics, when humans found from their observations a humility of a kind that had previously come only from their theories of a supernatural, they returned to a chaos in which they must nevertheless, with faith, play familiar games, or, as some of my friends would put it, they must still maintain sufficient pride to make action possible."

He then walked out. By running I caught him in the corridor. I asked him at once if he really had been the girl who had shared her body with mine. The man I thought of as the illusionist stared at me for a moment or two, then began walking down the corridor. I followed him, and he walked more quickly to avoid me. When I asked him if he *was* the illusionist he stared at me in curiosity, without answering, then walked even more quickly. In the end he handed me over to a guard, saying that I might need special attention. As he walked away he began to seem quite different from the illusionist, although in some ways still like him.

PART TWO

the prince

CHAPTER 6

the interpreters

I had been called again to the computer room. Banners with the slogan FREEDOM THROUGH PRIDE hung on its walls, but they could not hide what looked like bullet scars on the concrete. The cabinets of many of the computers were battered, and the metal fronts of several of them were slit open. Armed guards marched between them; men and women in long white coats stood in front of those that were still working. I was marched up to the place where I had gone through my first interrogation. An attendant explained that to make communication with the computers easier I was to receive their messages through interpreters. The man and woman who would do the interpreting turned their backs on me to face the machines.

Both computers clicked and flashed. A long, thin strip of paper with marks on it began to flow out of the red computer. The woman interpreter examined it. "I am to inform you," she said, "that the Prince's great rebellion has begun."

Studying the blankness of the paper that had come out of the black computer, the other interpreter interrupted: "The computers were among the first to declare their loyalty to the Prince's cause. They are fully confident in his victory."

"I am to inform you," said the woman, "that when the Prince's victory is assured a proposal will be put to you by the Prince himself. If you fail, the consequences are unimaginable. Your future mission is mentioned now to indicate that this interrogation is something more than a mere intellectual discussion. There are to be no questions."

Out of the black computer there came a card with symbols on it. The interpreter examined the symbols and said: "I am to remind you that in your initial interrogation you said that you were pulled alternatively between the desire to act and the desire to contemplate. As you may have acknowledged on your adventure with the beach community, most of your species can find meaning only in habit, but there is no consolation in habit for you, nor any interest in it for the Prince. It should have been obvious enough in your second adventure that of those who follow action, few think about it, and it should have been clear on your third adventure that of those who care for contemplation, many, if they devote their thinking to action, do not know the thing they are contemplating. It is because you both think and act, and scorn habit, that you are eligible for consideration by the Prince. These qualities are, of course, also characteristic of the Prince."

A card dropped out of the red computer. "I am also to inform you," said the interpreter, "that it was because you spoke of 'freedom and pride' in the same terms as the Prince that you have been chosen for this mission."

A card came out of the black computer. Its interpreter examined it and said: "You are to know . . ." He stopped, read the card again, then threw it into a rubbish bin. It fell face-up and I could read it clearly. It said: "Perhaps human aspiration must be based on the belief in Chaos and Death."

Both computers were silent. There was no more paper, but the interpreter of the red computer remained facing it. There was a faint click, and a sheet of paper dropped out.

74

She handed me the paper. On it were instructions to fly to a distant city, to report there to a certain person at a certain address, and to wait in the city for the outcome of the Prince's rebellion. The message printed under these instructions said: "The Prince's struggle will take many forms. It is in this city that you will discover whether the Prince achieves his final triumph, or whether he fails."

the young conspirator

Each time an insect died the violet light crackled. Streaked with this light, we stood on a terrace looking out on the glare of an artificial lake and the dark warmth of the night. It seemed as hot as midday, and as crowded. I had flown to the city, as directed by the computer; now I was impounded at the airport, along with some of the adventurers who had flown in, attracted by the city's disorders. Troops pointed rifles at us and an officer slowly checked our papers. Among the adventurers the talk was almost all of the city—of the trapped president, and of the four ministers who were conspiring to replace him. There was talk of rebellion in other cities, but no mention of the unimaginable rebellion of the Prince. The radio on the terrace spoke of the continuing decline in power of the president, now unable even to leave his palace except by helicopter to the hills.

When my papers were cleared I went off in a car to the destination I had been given. I had not known what to expect of the city, and I had not imagined its dilapidation. For miles from the airport it seemed patched out of rubbish. A wide, bare-earthed road cut through acres of humans' kennels made out of old timber, sides of packing-cases, rusted wire. Even in the established parts of the city most of the surface had worn off the roads. As we rattled past side-streets I saw women washing clothes in the brown water of old horse-troughs, and the bare arses of men hunched over street drains, shitting into them. It seemed not so much a city as bits of a city, thrust up at random here and there, with suburbs lapping around them. We passed along a sudden swell of boulevards, split down the middle and lined with trees. We roared through a back street; in its tree-fronted villas, crumbling and meshed with barbed wire, there were reminders of an earlier gracefulness.

Several times we passed great weedy spaces. In the centre of some of these stood clumps of new statuary; in others gleaming monuments sprouted. In one of them there was a triumphal arch, half built, on another a great arena, weeds growing up its walls; in the centre of a stretch of earth as muddy as a cattle yard there was a high building, almost all of glass, some of it broken; a street market had assembled in the mud at its base. We passed a great central square that was nothing but an expanse of coarse, unkempt grass, tufty with weeds. A high monument in white marble and silver was at its edge.

The driver slowed down as we passed along tree-lined streets of suburban villas set in fine gardens. Armoured cars stood on several of the neatly trimmed lawns, and guards had mounted heavy machine-guns among the clipped shrubs. Soldiers diverted us into nearby streets. We stopped at the entrance to a hotel.

The hotel was surrounded by the glitter of small bars and cafés, but its own lights had failed and only storm lanterns lit its lobby. I at once gained a key to a room from the reception clerk, who warned me to bolt my door. My room was large and polished, with its own lobby. There were patterned tiles on its floor, leather chairs, and a bed big enough to sleep five or six. When I tried to unwind the shutters, the handle fell off, and in the bathroom I found

77

that there was no water. The vast shabbiness of the room dissolved into familiar blackness when the candle went out. I woke only once; the shutters were rattling, there was a chopping of helicopters, and I seemed to hear the cracks and thuds of distant firing.

Now holding the handle more carefully, I unwound the shutters and looked down at the traffic roundabout below. Around a fountain that was a monument to human brotherhood there flowed a stream of jeeps, sedans, troop carriers, buses, army trucks, bicycles, tanks, field guns. On the steel skeleton of a tall unfinished building a huge hoarding proclaimed a new belief. Inside my room there were other notices: FLIP THE ORANGE SWITCH TO TURN THE RADIO ON . . . NECKTIES SHOULD BE WORN IN THE GARDENIA ROOM AT ALL TIMES . . . I turned on the radio: just before dawn there had been a massacre in one of the suburbs; a guerrilla hideout had been discovered and the whole guerrilla force had been killed. The mutilated corpses found freshly buried in the garden of the guerrilla headquarters were the bodies of some of the city's great men, who had been seized in their houses several days before. The radio called on the president to establish his innocence of their murder.

Death had been restored to our existence! For ever? Or until the contest was resolved? The disorder released by the Prince's distant and mysterious struggle had given back to us the greatest of our uncertainties. My lungs ached as I felt them snatch at the air, busy in their trivial cause. I could pick up the knife from my breakfast tray, greasy with animal fat, and hack the life out of my throat.

Five military trucks were passing in convoy outside. In them I saw my old comrades of the encampments, stiff and straight, their faces gravely gentle. What would happen to them now? The radio crackled with reports of attacks and counter-attacks in some of the city's provinces, deaths from starvation in the slums and among the camps of adventurers who had settled outside the city. Now that we could kill again, would we have done with ourselves altogether? There was an advertisement for a brand of toothpaste, then the announcer opened a discussion between two students and two professors on the relations between the generations.

In the street there seemed a freshness even in the mud. Everything seemed changed now that we could die again. As I walked from a boulevard into a suburban street, going to the address I had been given, a limousine bumped past, kicking up its rump like a horse. Riding in it was the marshal. His fat cheeks were pink with pleasure. His medals were jingling.

I went into a courtyard shady with ferns. It was filled with men puffing scented cigarettes, serious-faced, speaking softly as if waiting for me to leave so that they could talk more openly. Fireworks exploded in the garden, lighting up their faces. Only one of them was sitting, the youngest there, but received with deference by all the others. Each time the telephone rang he would leave the courtyard, shout into the telephone with confidence, then return and finish what he had been saying. There was something familiar in his fine nose and strong shoulders, his proud stare, his apparent grace and strength. He seemed to have the inhuman beauty of a statue. He did not hide his arrogance.

He called me over and spoke to me softly, as if for his own amusement. Then, with a gesture so unexpectedly elaborate that it must have been ironic, he led me into a small room in the house. "I shall try to make some sense of this for you," he said. The straddling of his legs denied some of his appearance of confidence. "We are going through probably the greatest of our periodic stages of revolt. Supporters of the Prince—if this is what they really are—have seized the computer hall and other important establishments, and some that are not so important—easy things, merely taken to impress. There is revolt in all existence. The affairs of this city play some part in this general

79

turning-over of everything—I am not sure how; perhaps even the Prince does not know—but I am sent here as a spy and a conspirator. In some way the overthrow of the president plays a part in the victory of the Prince. As a spy, I know what to do: I send back reports that the situation is extremely confused, and give examples. But as a conspirator, what can I do? There is no exact answer. I support this and that . . . I scheme here and there . . . and in my reports I take credit for whatever happens that seems to favour the overthrow of the president and, presumably, the cause of the Prince."

Through a window I saw the men in the courtyard form up and march off. There was a sound of rifle shots. Farther off there was the crack of a field gun and the thump of an exploding shell. "Among others, I have conspired with the students," said the young conspirator. "That is what one is supposed to do now, isn't it? But I am sure my connections with them have no particular effect, except to allow me, in my reports, to take credit for their successes. Come with me now, and I'll show you an example of what I mean."

On the square in front of the president's palace the horde of students seemed to expand and contract like a sea monster: their shouts bubbled up, then there was silence. One young man was shrieking: when they all took up his cry and rolled towards the railings the soldiers raised their machine-guns and fired at the sky; spent cartridge cases rattled on the pavement. Two tanks moved delicately into the square and stood quietly. The students fell back from the railings, their ranks again rhythmically expanding and contracting; then they were still, as if their breathing had stopped. After an army commander addressed them they formed into a long column and marched off, chanting derision. When they had gone the soldiers laughed, and several of them jeered at the president through the railings.

We had been watching these tableaux from a window

fronting the square. "That kind of thing goes down well in a report," said the young conspirator. "Now we'll talk to a couple of the real leaders of the students and find out what they think has been happening."

The first of the leaders was living in a villa seized from a discredited supporter of the president. Its furniture had been smashed and thrown into a heap in the garden. We stood for a while on a veranda among the young rebel's guards, then moved under escort through the bare room, at the end of which the young man sat, stiff and stern in a torn cane chair; beside him, on the floor, were tumbled bed-clothes. On the table there was a pistol. He waved to us to sit below him, then harangued us for a quarter of an hour on the meaning of honour. His thin wrists and little hands flicked like an insect's. He pulled from a pocket three torn pages of a notebook from which he read a manifesto of his policy for the city, written that morning and not yet pro-claimed. He gave us five slogans, numbering each of them. He looked up. "Number six," he said. "The extermination of the president." He flicked a wrist at us and rose.

In a pavilion in the garden of another of the seized villas we met the second of the young rebel leaders. He sat on his bed, eyes appealing sadly to us from a long, triangu-lar face, but lips grinning with hope. He spoke so quietly and quickly that my attention went more towards the books scattered around his room, the slogans scrawled on the walls, the dirty plates and ashtrays filled with butts. When he began to speak of the president a rainstorm burst on us so that I heard nothing of what he said, judging it only by the gentleness of his smile. As he reached the end of his oration a pipe broke and water cannonaded outside on an empty drum.

Over dinner the young conspirator explained that in his report he would say that the student movement was divided between revolutionaries and reformists: the first of the two student leaders could be fitted into the first category, although he doubted if this leader would ever kill anything except time; like me, because of the noise of the rain, he had not heard what the second student leader had said, but he *looked* a reformist, and, even if he wasn't, no doubt some other student leader was.

"You may think me indifferent to the fate of the Prince's great struggle," he said, leaning back in his chair. "But this is not so. The fate of the Prince is all that matters to me. He is my being and I have served him throughout existence. When his last great revolt failed the results were disastrous for tens of thousands of us, but what would my existence be except in his service? On this occasion we may again be lost. But if I can still serve the Prince in defeat, then even defeat has its reward."

When I asked him why, then, he was so cynical in the Prince's service he said: "It is not in the Prince's service that I am cynical, but—as with the Prince himself—in the service of history. Whether I should conspire one way or the other—whether conspiracy matters at all—seems so uncertain that most of my decisions might as well be taken by chance. As for my lying reports—the Prince won't waste time on any of them; they are merely for the satisfaction of some of his lesser and more naive officials."

After dinner we drove along a wide highway that carried us in long crescents and loops into an even wider highway. The young conspirator gave me the names of various buildings as we passed them—some had already been renamed by the president's opponents—and for no reason I saw him as a friend, whose knowledge of adventure mocked even his sense of loyalty. He interrupted himself with something he appeared to believe might trouble me. "As you know, our revolts are echoes of your own revolts, which themselves are echoes of a myriad complex things." He gave a slight frown. "But wouldn't it be wonderful if we could still believe that the Prince rides above history, omnipotent past the limit of our imagination? Of course,

82

among many of his new followers, we are already generating that fiction." I noticed for the first time that his hands were red and rough, with thick wrists.

He took me to one of the receptions that were now being given. All the talk was of the high politics and the great men of the city. Most of it was the latest gossip of the president, still twisting and turning in the prison of his palace. Several nights before he had held a ball to which he had invited even the four ministers who were moving patiently to depose him, and for an evening they had laughed together. He continued to call for plans for new monuments, welcome visitors, proclaim slogans, strike paragraphs out of letters, or declaim on the secrets of existence, but the instructions he sent to the ministries were ignored.

The young conspirator had decided to spend no more time on the students. They could be expected to be active in any case, he said; reports therefore could still be made on their actions, and credit taken for them. But there had been complaints that he was ignoring the elites of the city, so for the next fortnight we went, afternoon and night, to receptions. The city paid homage to the president by its gossip, even if it was the gossip of his overthrow. The mere mention that a certain minister or a famous general had seen him privately was enough to set off an evening's anxiety. On the hour he was to make a speech there was no entertainment to be had in the city. I listened to the speech with the conspirator, admiring the warmth and charm of the voice elaborating nothingness. At the reception afterwards it was agreed that the speech was a failure. The revolution could now proceed. Men discussed plans for purging the ministries. They compared lists of those who should be exiled or gaoled.

What would they do? Send some soldiers to the president's palace and shoot him? Have done with him in a few minutes, leaving a carcass among the scattered documents and smashed treasures? Or drain the magic out of him by putting him on trial? Frighten him into some general confession of his errors? Or could they keep him, although naked of power, as a face on the coinage and a symbol of state? Could he be dismissed somewhere among the cross-purposes and loud debates of the Assembly? But the Assembly was still filled with his creatures. Most preferred more intricate manoeuvres, to bluff him into abdicating his power in the name of the people and handing on its strength to his successor. He had to be frightened and coaxed into action, not destroyed. If he were destroyed, nothing would be sacred.

All I saw of the four ministers was the buildings of their ministries, each in a different part of the city, each in its character. To these buildings the ministers swept through the streets each day, each in his own procession of steel, and then, alone in the compounds of power, they were said to concern themselves most with each other. When they returned to their villas at night it was to gardens planted with armoured cars and machine-gun posts and blazing lights.

We would check the points of the ministers as if they were horses. Theatrical qualities: tick; tick; cross; tick. Support in the provinces: cross; tick; tick; cross. Appeal to the army: tick; cross; cross; tick. Towards the end of a reception, after the confidence of checking lists, there might be a rumour that this very night the admirals had all set out to sea, planning a revolt in the president's favour; or that the closest adviser of one of the ministers had been seen that day with a loyal friend of the president; or that the northern province would revolt in two days' time.

I met the four ministers only when the conspirator was given instructions that he was to concentrate his activities entirely on the ministers and their entourages. For some days I saw him hardly at all. Then he said that it would serve his interest—and perhaps provide me with some diversion—if he could introduce me to each of the ministers as a distinguished and influential stranger. He said he wished to observe their reactions to this situation.

The first minister was small, with a big head. He lay back in his chair, not moving. His voice was so low that I could hear him less clearly than the click of the soldiers' boots in the corridor. The room was dark, but a desk light was cast in such a way that the minister's head seemed to glow. His body remained still; his only movement was an occasional fluttering of the fingers. He spoke quickly of the sufferings of the people and then showed nimbleness in sketching the political games of the city, even making some reference to the manoeuvrings of the Prince. But out of these events he seemed also to be trying to weave some pattern of goodness. He was already prepared to see nobility in the failure of his own revolt and that of the Prince. He spoke with disdain of killing, and with love of the failings of the president. He spoke much of honour, a matter to which he seemed to give great calculation.

The second of the ministers strode across his room to shake my hand; holding it lightly, with his other hand on my shoulder, he led me to a conference of his advisers. Young, sharp, lively, he looked at me with intelligence. Whenever I asked him a question, he cocked his head and stared at me with eyebrows raised politely. When I had finished asking a question he merely nodded, as if congratulating me, and then, cocking his head into a question mark, turned it to each of his advisers. When each of them answered he said nothing, merely pecking his head at them in acknowledgment. When all the answers were given he motioned towards the adviser whose answer he most preferred, and repeated it to me. The answer he chose was always the most general and most meaningless.

The third minister received me in a large room, shouting to me from a distance as he walked from one window to the next, striking a pose at each, like a statue in a niche. Arms akimbo, eyes flashing, he proclaimed, with a hero's vigour, the virtues of the pragmatic and the ordinary. Like the first minister, he saw both the Prince's revolt and his own as part of the same thing: not because of the honour to be found in it, but because of its "practical benefits". Sitting at a table and reading from a list, he outlined the most important of these expected benefits at some length. It seemed unlikely that so many changes and advantages could be expected to spring from one single action. In the romance and sentiment with which he idealised his practicality he seemed lacking in shrewdness, showing less calculation than the first minister had shown in the pursuit of honour.

Smiling only slightly, as if not to boast too much about it, the fourth minister led me to a chair beside a window and, with the gentleness of a big man, asked my advice on some small matters. Resting his chin on his strong hands, he spoke of his lack of cleverness. Keeping his brown eyes on mine, he told me anecdotes of the intelligence of the president and of the other three ministers. Like an old man seeking a young body, he seemed to want to warm himself against the cleverness of others, and he spoke of the great care his advisers must bear if destiny elected him successor to the president. After telling me some simple stories of his childhood, he placed a firm hand on my shoulder and led me to the door, pausing to say that to serve a cause well a man must follow his conscience and that it was in this above all that he put trust in the Prince.

"Well, what did you make of them?" I was at dinner with the young conspirator. I began to answer, but before I could finish he handed me a coin. After three tosses he declared the winner.

The food was tentative and dispirited, and the young conspirator was morose. He suggested that we discuss possible meanings of the events of which we were witnesses and, for all we knew, participants. I said that perhaps through the distant and unknown struggle of the Prince, it had become a time for change. Would the fate of both president and Prince be settled by the fashion of the age? The young conspirator went on eating. He said nothing more than that his cynicism was itself an excuse for his involvement in action: perhaps he had to believe that there could be some sense or purpose in individual decisions, even if there was not. In the meantime he would do his best.

Having expressed himself with such detachment, he seemed, by the next day, and for the first time in our acquaintance, to take on with belief his role as conspirator. Something had concerned him in the latest instructions he had received, and even in conversation with me he seemed ready to act, or to pretend to act, as if he thought there was some way in which he might after all affect events. He still insisted on taking me with him, and in a brief return to his old manner he said that he wanted me present so that I could affirm that he had done this or that; if it should happen to become connected with later events, I could then stand witness; if it didn't, we could laugh about it later. Then, in a different mood from any I had previously detected in him, he said that events in the city—and perhaps also in the affairs of the Prince—now seemed to be reaching their climax and that at such a time there should be an end to fooling around, because choice and action became possible.

The first of his three attempts at more orthodox conspiratorial methods occurred at one of the evening receptions. We were talking to a fat little general who, sweating with joviality, told us about a garden party he was planning for the following week. Disguising his usual predilection to impress, the young conspirator began, diffidently, to lead the general into a discussion of his guest list and from that, with many diversions and anecdotes, to a consideration of inviting to the party the most important adviser of each of the four ministers. In several half-finished sentences and a few interpolatary anecdotes he brought home the point that these four advisers had never met each other. The general told us that he would bring them together, and explained to us how clever this idea of his was.

The next night, in the composing-room of a newspaper office, where writers worked at failing typewriters among the printing machinery because there was no room for them elsewhere, an editor stood at the printer's stone where type was beginning to assemble around the edges of a forme, and after discussing for a time some breakdown in the machinery, told us of the editorial that would appear in the next day's paper if the machinery could be patched together in time. The young conspirator began to discuss the editorial with him, asking stupid questions about a phrase here and there. He did all of this so haltingly that, in correcting the conspirator's mistakes, the editor gave the editorial a quite different meaning. When this farce was over, the editor assured us that we were about to witness the end of tyranny and the beginning of freedom for us all. He spoke of how all the powerful men in the city would read his editorial at breakfast and be heartened by it, and finally take courage.

The next day the young conspirator told me that his latest manoeuvre would have to be carried out secretly, but that he hoped to display its success to me that night. After dinner he took me off in his car, driving through streets I had not seen before. In one of them I heard the kind of cry a man makes only when he feels some new pain. A young soldier, fresh-faced and handsome, was standing on the pavement with laconic grace, lifting his boot now and again to kick the head of a man in the gutter. The door of the house behind him was open; lights blazing inside showed soldiers ransacking it; other soldiers stood on the pavement, as elegant as statues. For the first time the young conspirator seemed to see a connection between what he had done and what later happened. He told me that he had urged some

88

cleansing of the adventurers who had come to the city. At least in this one case he had succeeded. The fat body that kicked and twisted in the gutter was that of the marshal.

Perhaps because even the young conspirator himself now seemed to attach some significance to his actions, I became extremely bored with the political affairs of the city. I refused his company, preferring to walk in the streets, where the poor displayed their degradation. I would walk until I was lost, then find my way back to my hotel so tired that I would fall asleep in my clothes, and wake in the morning to see in the mirror parts of a stranger's body. The radio still crackled with news, but I began to doubt whether it would matter to the people in the streets whether they were governed by the president or by one of the four ministers. They were men contending for power, and therefore they affronted the hopes of those I saw in the streets. I tried to imagine what excitement might come to me if the Prince triumphed, but I knew that even a victory for the Prince might make little difference to the people in the streets.

One night rockets slipped into the sky while in the square outside the hotel a crowd pressed and yelled. Assuming that this demonstration was yet another manoeuvre prompted by one of the ministers, I went to sleep. But when the young conspirator burst in with the morning, I learned that the rockets had heralded the end of tyranny. The president was overthrown. The fourth minister would that day be proclaimed president. The young conspirator was both pleased, and sceptical of his pleasure. He said that a case might be made for suggesting that the president's overthrow was, among other things, the result of the bringing-together of the four ministers' advisers by the fat general, the effects of the heroic message of the newspaper editor, and the unity that had come from the agreement to expel the marshal and some of the other adventurers. He did not believe that this was so, but it would be difficult to disprove it. In his report he intended to suggest that it was by *his* actions that the president had been overthrown. The Prince would laugh at such a childish idea, but he would understand that it was part of our nature to look for a cause in things and that if this explanation were put on record quickly enough it might later become accepted as an important piece of evidence.

We went off in the young conspirator's car, sending the litter flying, pretending that everything was as bright as the clear light of the morning. Tens of thousands of people already crowded the squares around the president's palace, shouting out a new hope. Even the blue of the sky and the sparkle of the air seemed renewed. As our car rushed down the great highway, children laughed and ran; families were on excursion; young people paired off. In their holiday clothes, with flags flapping and balloons bobbing above their heads, the crowds flew past gracefully. Among them gleamed the ceremonial drums with which they were to greet the new president. At one intersection, five peacocks flaunted their tails. At another, white horses pranced in a carnival.

All along the highway the drums were sounding, quick, precise, confident. We stopped and listened to the thunder behind us and ahead of us. Arms flashed, backs strained, legs were taut. An artillery salute was fired. Aircraft swooped. A crowd roared.

In the helicopter the young conspirator said that the Prince had instructed him to tell me three things. First, the Prince knew that he himself should now be taking me to a high mountain to show me all existence in its glory, but since his cares still detained him the conspirator instead was to play this part, and since there was no place near by—perhaps anywhere—from which all existence could be observed, a helicopter trip over the city would have to do. "Now," said the conspirator, "do what the Prince says." I looked down at the city and admired the smallness of the hope with which it thrust itself up towards us.

Second, the conspirator had to ask me to consider the excitements of power over even a small part of so much activity; I was also to remember that since the possibilities of progress were as great as those of reaction, there could always be some good in it for others if not for myself. If change was possible, it must have its agents. Why should I not be one of them?

We dropped sideways, swooping on a city square as if to seize one of those who were standing there cheering and carry him off with us, kicking and yelling; we cut through the air above roofs, then began twisting upwards again, then sideways, out across villages and open country. On the horizon there was another city, spread along a coast.

The conspirator turned to me and shouted his third instruction. I was to consider whether, with such great changes occurring, I could merely stand by with no sense of choice?

It was dark by now, and I saw the conspirator's face by the cabin lights. He asked if I would join the Prince's cause. What words came into my head came falsely. I simply said, "Yes."

The conspirator then told me that on this day not only had the president been deposed; the Prince had also gained his mysterious victory. He turned the helicopter and we were soon flying over the sea, towards the victorious Prince.

CHAPTER 8

the conscience of the prince

We landed at dawn. Boots clicked and arms were flung up in salutes. Sirens wailing, our car swept in an arc around a green hill and on to a white highway which seemed to pull us forward at once into greater speed. We shot over a long, graceful bridge, and along a processional way flanked by tall white columns whose tops had been blown off. At the end of it was a large white structure with many silver domes. Before our eyes the structure shook, and exploded into a cloud of rubble and dust. The young conspirator explained that a certain amount of demolition work had to be done. Soon we were rushing through open countryside. The building in which we would find the functionary whom the young conspirator called "the Chief" seemed to slam against our eyes when we stopped.

The ground floor was being turned, with great bustle, into a planning hall. Vast electrically operated maps and charts were being screwed into the golden marble and across the sunlit glass; steel conference tables and filing-cabinets were being scraped along the floors. Strung from one side of the hall to the other, a huge banner proclaimed: BROTHERS! WE ARE EQUALLY FREE! Soldiers stood on guard at each end of it.

We passed through a large room in which hundreds of men were bustling over charts and diagrams. Some of the window glass had been smashed, and there were bullet marks on the walls. A banner hung at one end carrying the words: FREEDOM—OR SERVILITY? In an empty hall littered with paper, its chairs disarranged and its wall ornaments stripped off, there were two banners. One said: WHO CAN THINK SUBMISSION? The other: HONOUR! GLORY! RENOWN!

As the young conspirator took me up a small set of stairs he said that it was in this building that the details of my "expedition" were to be settled. We stood outside the door of a small room. The conspirator explained that, preferring the ostentation of modesty, "the Chief" had chosen this room as his office because it was the smallest in the building.

The story-teller opened the door and let us in. He asked the young conspirator to wait outside and went back to the window where he had been standing. In the light blue hills in the distance artillery shells were bursting. "Detail!" he said. "I watch it, but I don't know why it's happening. It is almost certainly some act of idiocy." He sat behind his desk, his grey eyes still on the window. "Perhaps it is one of the essentials of leadership that the leader should accept idiocies among his subordinates without inquiring too much into them. If he tries to know everything he learns nothing. Only a fool should concern himself overmuch with idiots, and a great man can hire fools for this very purpose."

He seemed at once to regret the harshness of what he had said, adding that he did not speak from his own experience. For all that he was now known as "the Chief" of this particular establishment, he had never felt more removed from greatness; his role was probably more that of a hired jester than of a great man. He spoke for a while of the cleansing punishment of his predicament since he had all the appearance of power and none of its substance. It had not occurred to him before what abasement there must be for those who outwardly display the arrogance of high office but daily learn its secret humiliations. He said he was little more than a monument and did not doubt that, like the emblems that had been blown off the white monoliths in the processional way, he could be as easily removed if policy demanded it. He sought nothing for himself but his own failure, although he must take care not to achieve his cleansing at the expense of others, or find vanity in it.

Drinks were brought in, and after toasting what he described as my forthcoming voyage the story-teller asked if I had any questions. I asked where my voyage was to take me.

"To Earth," he said, smiling at me a little.

To what purpose?

"That is a matter of detail," he said. "It is only in my kind of ambiguous position that one can really avoid detail, for the very good reason that no one tells me anything."

Why had I been chosen for this mission?

"A matter of whim," said the story-teller. "As soon as I reported that you had seen a connection between pride and freedom, the Prince seized on it. He made much of the accident that you had used a slogan he was playing with. He used it against colleagues who opposed him as we would once have used what at that time we called 'a sign'."

He said my interview with him was merely a formality to give dignity to the occasion and since his dignity was in much demand he would soon pass me on to lesser officials. In the meantime he wished me luck.

As I was walking to the door, I asked him what powers I would possess when I returned to Earth.

"Because of the speed with which matters are being decided," he said, "the best you can do is to go off on your journey as quickly as possible and assume that when you get there you will discover by some means what powers you have been given."

Outside, an official, directing his question at a point somewhere above my head, asked me to name three people I would choose to see on Earth. I chose a comrade who had been with me in the trenches, the son the computer had told me about and whichever one of my grandsons was closest to my own physical age. In using the words "son" and "grandson" I felt as if I was speaking on behalf of some stranger who had asked me to deliver a message.

The white of the room in which the young official received me dazzled like a surgeon's theatre. He apologised for what he described as the melodrama of what was about to occur. His instructions were that my journey to the Prince was to remain mysterious to me; there was some talk of security, but he was sure that the demand for mystery was mainly a matter of habit. Since the journey was a long one he could not merely blindfold me; at the same time he did not wish to employ the traditional theatricality. To maintain the illusion of contemporaneity he would use a chemical injection. He asked me to take off my jacket and roll up a sleeve.

The room in which I awoke seemed to be some kind of exhibition hall. I was lying on a stretcher in the middle of it, surrounded by the exhibits. The young conspirator was sitting watching me.

"It's the kind of thing we have to try out," he said. "Several floors of this building are devoted to propaganda exhibits. This morning they were all rejected out of hand. The Prince has not seen them, but since he has insisted that there should not be a mere *bouleversement* of the traditional, the officials here, for safety's sake, reject everything. In any case, how can anyone decide anything until the Prince himself knows what he will do now that he has won? Of course there is the New Belief the computers are working on, but they haven't decided yet what it is. We're doing what always happens—slap something together, good and bad, wisdom and absurdities, and off we rush, waving our banners." As we were leaving the room, he said: "This time some of us had hoped better of the Prince. But I suppose he is quite likely to press out an improvisation of something that is better than the computers could produce with all their speculative dawdling."

As we walked along a corridor the young conspirator glanced at me several times, and once smiled in half-apology. A lift took us up with a rush that pressed on my ears. Dozens of numbers flicked across its indicator panel. We got out at what seemed the top of the building, stepping into a huge hall with walls of glass. Through the glass I saw below us a walled city, all in white, set out in a plain full of flowers, with blue lakes sparkling on the horizon. Under the mild light of the sky I saw the silver sand of two rivers lined with trees. The sun's rays burst into the gold of domes and spires, and silver bells rang out; fountains cascaded and glittered, spraying above the marble of the city's squares; grapevines glistened among the slender pillars of white terraces and courtyards; wide open parks were interlaced with walled gardens; and above everything there rose, on white columns, monuments of gold.

"Go a little closer to it," said the young conspirator. When I looked at the glass close-up there was a flatness, even a coarseness, in the images of the city. Arranged to give the illusion of perspective, shapes suggesting a city had been inserted one behind another between layers of glass. We went through a small door near the lift, down some steps and into a long room where some guards sat. There we waited for some word from the Prince.

Eventually we were led into a small, humble room with bare walls. We sat beneath a window in one corner. Like all the other windows in this building, it had an illusion constructed into its glass: this one was of night, with the shapes of other buildings suggested in shadows. The young conspirator laughed and said that he assumed

I would not regard such childishness as being of any significance. I forgot about it when the Prince came into the room.

There was both thunder and brightness about the Prince. As he talked to the young conspirator I saw that in his gestures he was proudly eminent, but when he rested, listening, care sat on his forehead, made up of both ruthlessness and remorse. Although he was clothed, I seemed to see him dauntlessly naked, bold and proud, courageous and defiant. I wanted to throw myself at his feet and to babble at him that my greatest hope was to be accepted, like the young conspirator, into his companionship.

He turned to me and said: "When I was vain and envious they saw me as glorious and benign. It was only when I took on my cares for humanity that they turned me into a cartoon. They saw me with twisted horns, a goat's beard, and satyr's legs. They put a second face in my belly and gave me three fiery heads. I snarled with dog's teeth. My chest was heavy with bitch's breasts. Bats wings flapped from my back. And I was supposed to swish a barbed tail." He rose and a brief bitterness seized him. "When I ate, I ate sinners. When I breathed, I breathed out toads and scorpions." He sat down again and smiled. "They cast me in the shape of their fears. It was themselves they made ridiculous."

He was silent, and his silence was itself a command. He rested his chin on his hand. Then he said gently: "Imagine a beach of burning sand beside an ocean of flame. It is fed by a fetid, stinking river. Imagine behind the beach that there are black and smoky marshes running into a dark wood filled with bandits and angry dogs and rustling with bats and owls, ravens and triple-headed beasts. See above it, between the rolling clouds of smoke, the green light of a malignant moon. Imagine inland seas of boiling pitch, scalding geysers, sulphurous volcanoes, and violent shakings of the earth. Think for a moment of the raucous factory

97

quarters where, in lawns of nettles and thistles, the furnaces roar and black fire shoots out of the pits.

"Then imagine the tortures: the floggings by bullock-balled monsters, the bird-beaked demons picking at flesh; the adulterous hanging by their hair from trees while snakes crawl in the men's guts and toads suck at the women's breasts; the suicides impaled on stakes from arse to gullet, the eyes eaten by worms, the genitals shrivelled in molten lead; the running sores, emaciations, rapes and eviscerations, the brains boiling in the skull, the banquets of shit, the monsters exhaling the embers of burnt souls, the heaps of rotting flesh, the trickle of blood from torn bowels, the brilliant colours of the viscera. And then of all this tedious horror imagine me the chief commandant." He looked at me as if testing the degree of my attention, and went on even more softly:

"Then imagine the calm faces of the damned as they wait in line for their turn, naked, but still modestly concealing their genitals. Or imagine their faces, still serious with responsibility and care, as they stand silently and thoughtfully in the middle of the flames. Or imagine their calm innocence as they swing quietly from the trees, their intestines hanging down for the dogs to squabble over. Imagine a new batch arriving, great thinkers and men of affairs among them, all in chains, being led to the cauldrons calm and confident, even proud, as if in a procession that was proclaiming their own victory." He again looked at me as if testing my attention, then simply walked out of the room, taking the young conspirator with him. All he said was "Stay here and think about that."

For half an hour or so I tried to turn the bare walls of the room into tapestries of horror. When the Prince came back he took up his speech as if he had merely paused to cough.

"How could humans go on suffering if they knew that existence was to hold nothing but suffering? What could they do when faced by an infinity of absurd torments? They could *laugh!* They could become humorously self-righteous against the evil of such tedious persecutors." For the first time he showed sorrow. "Consider the tormentors themselves. If they were beings of some aspiration, mightn't they grow to love a species that could accept such insults so calmly?"

He attended to some matters of business, signing some papers and sending them off. Then he looked up again and said: "There was a further complexity! The tests of judgement were not related to the potential of the species. Some of the humble people escaped—they were humble in their hopes and therefore not damned—but the tests were so unreal that *all* of those who were engaged in thought or took responsibility towards events were sent to the carnival of tortures. Every one of them! There was not one thinker, not one man of action, who did not become a guest of the tormentors!"

He paused. "How could we take seriously such a system in which it was necessarily evil that anyone should concern himself with the conduct of affairs, or think about them?" He paused again. "Perhaps it is so—perhaps to act or to think *is* to fall below aspiration. But does this necessarily mean that only the bad should think or act? Or is it possible that honour can be found in the decision to debase oneself by accepting such a responsibility?" He again left the room.

I spent the day with the young conspirator, waiting in one anteroom after another for some word that the Prince was to see us again. When at last we were called to him he was in a committee room, waiting between one meeting and the next. He spoke with less force than before, for a moment putting his arm around me as he sat me down at the long table. Then he said, as if puzzled and asking my advice: "If there is to be no more immortality, how must a man face death?"

He gave me a cup of coffee. "It used to be a kind of artistic performance to suffer life with fortitude and death with valour. A man could be satisfied in his life by being his own audience. Now men merely feel petulant. They feel robbed of their cultural nurturing—which was that they should possess individual souls—so they sulk about it. Some of them continue the old practices, but, not having souls, they now try to save their bodies. They mortify their carcasses with exercises, they make confessions to lay specialists, they fast in health camps or on diets. They are still looking for some physical metaphor for those hopes of perfection that no human will ever possess."

"Except for a few of the mad," said the young conspirator.

"And even they can now sometimes be cured of it," said the Prince.

I dined alone with the young conspirator. At first he gossiped about the absurdities of many of the Prince's new supporters. "Some of those of most renown have supported each new belief in turn," he said, "somehow surviving as, in turn, each belief fails. The Prince doesn't trust them, but he must deal with them, and his instructions are that the rest of us emigrés must let them lord it over us for a while." Then he told me some stories of the weaknesses of the Prince, speaking with love, as if it were necessary for loyalty to the Prince that I should know his imperfections.

Towards the end of the evening we were called to yet another conference room. On our way to it the young conspirator said: "What is being worked on now, with its general basis in the acceptance of death as oblivion, exactly fits the heroic caste of mind of the Prince. The irony, as you have no doubt observed, is that success for this belief would mean the annihilation of us all, including the Prince." Before we entered the conference room he said: "Perhaps the Prince would now welcome an end to his anxieties and labours. This is a favour that only your species can give us.

But, given its totality, it is a matter that for the Prince represents not only release but revenge."

The hall was crowded with people standing and listening to the Prince. He had reached his peroration:

"The more usual weapon of power is trickery, but its final weapon must always be slaughter. Why not acknowledge this? Do not deny violence but embrace it, and control it! Can there not, in the exercise of power, be a morality of violence? When to use it? How to use it? If from time to time men must degrade their humanity, can they not at least do it honourably and moderately? Equally, since power is not possible without cheating—when you cheat, know that you are cheating your own species. Why not accept this and produce a morality of fraudulence? If you are at least to some extent satisfied with the honour of the cause you serve, be no more dishonourable in its service than its success demands. Perhaps it is only in distinguishing one immorality from the other that morality can exist.

"Consider also how farcical power is. To act is to clown. To attempt to bring aspiration into effect is to be a fool. Almost everything there is to say about power has already been written, and some of the best of it by comic writers. Yet not to be ready to be a clown is to reject aspiration. Recognise your humanity! Do not expect too much of yourselves! You should learn pity for those who wield power, and you should learn compassion for power's most shocking characteristics."

The Prince walked abruptly out of the room and I did not see him again until the next night. This time we were summoned to an even larger conference room. The Prince walked up and down as he spoke. He said: "Having spoken of men of action, I shall speak now of men of thought. Reflect at first on the fact that many clever men sacrifice themselves, either deliberately or in illusion, to the manufacture of lies: in this era, in every community, although in one community they may serve a different purpose from the one

101

they serve in another, there are great factories set up for the planned production of falsehoods and sophistries. It may be true that the sense of humour of the ordinary people finally protects them from the more absurd products of these factories, but think of the destruction in honour and self-regard of those who are employed to make lies. Think of their terrors at losing their petty bribes, the affronts daily offered to their vanity, their sorrows in defeat and their fears in victory.

"This is the era of decision, of hordes of clever men with nimble, orderly wits sitting at desks and planning each day more changes than sometimes occurred before in a hundred years. At times the world seems to tremor with their brains. Yet also reflect on the profound silliness of so much of this cleverness: it throws up great pens of humans, tens of thousands strong, who can display most of the honourable characteristics of striving and dedication, but in the service of matters that you would regard as being of the utmost banality. By this means they, too, destroy their honour."

He ceased walking and stood near one of the false windows. "Chaos and Death! To recognise these is now where honour lies. To accept chaos, but not to be destroyed by it! To know that the species is limited in its perceptions of events, that its view of things must always be partial, distorted, tentative, inadequate, but nevertheless to risk accepting the faith without which freedom cannot exist. And accept death without losing belief! In the brotherhood of the species and in individual style find again that pride which gives existence its honour and without which—again —freedom cannot exist."

The Prince left the hall. A messenger told me that I was to join him at supper. When I arrived I found the young conspirator already there. They were sitting at a wooden table before some simple refreshment of a thin kind of biscuit and some wine. For a while they talked of

102

matters of immediate business, then the Prince spoke to me again, simply and even with a slight hesitation. He said: "Since we have no time I shall speak to you of only one of my purposes, although it is one of the most grand. I want to feel through you the texture of our New Belief. I want you to feel for yourself matters that even I cannot perhaps imagine, so that, given the experience I grant you on Earth, you will be ready, and quickly, for the role I shall then disclose to you. Be determined and you will find glory. Discover yourself in your brothers and your brothers in yourself."

He laughed, talked briefly to the young conspirator, and then returned to me. "You must excuse the inadequacies of these slogans," he said. "We still have people working on them. However, I can assure you that when your time comes you will be fully equipped with catch-cries and illustrative anecdotes. These will be the mere bunting and confetti of the New Belief, but such things are necessary. The general idea seems clear enough to me, including its dilemmas. All your species can be is human; yet you despise yourselves for your humanity. Know it and love it! But with its paradoxes: if you accept only its herdishness, you lose one of your two most noble characteristics; if you reject altogether the commonness among you and proclaim only individual vanity you lose the other. Your species must proclaim a pride in both brotherhood and individuality, and from this pride will come its freedom."

He broke off again and turned to the young conspirator. "Brotherhood and Individuality? Pride and Freedom?"

"No, I don't think so," said the young conspirator. He thought for a moment and then suggested: "Individuality through Brotherhood? Freedom through Pride?"

The Prince shook his head. "Find freedom in your brothers and they will find freedom in you?" He paused. "No," he said, "that has a different meaning."

They were both silent, then the young conspirator

said: "These are two different concepts. It may be impossible to put them together in a few words."

"Well, then," said the Prince, "perhaps we should change the concepts." He broke off. A tremor of impatience seized him and he again turned to me. "I display before you my inadequacies," he said. "Perhaps this is part of it. You must learn to find imperfection in everything, but still glory in what you are."

He stood up. "Trust me. I might fail. I am imperfect. But support our cause with valour. If I fail, I am doomed. I shall again bear the guilt of so many other miseries." He walked to the false window and stood for a while silent. As had happened at the beginning of his other speeches, and in a manner that held for me some unrecognised memory, his arm flicked towards me and stayed, momentarily still. He said: "If we succeed, you shall be our prophet!" He touched a ring he wore, of a serpent wrought in gold, then he gestured good-bye.

In the dark room to which he led me the young conspirator said that I must now think of death, of my own death on the beach. I must think of it with such purpose that nothing else existed: I must imagine that I was willing myself to die.

It was dark. I was cold. Blood was choking my nostrils. I was lying on the beach. There was vomit in my mouth. The rifles were still crackling in the hills. They were strapping my body to a raft. I was floating out, alone, into the mists of the sea.

PART THREE

*the lion, the fox
and the unicorn*

PART TWO

CHAPTER 9

the journey

I seemed to be floating across a dark sea, cold and in pain, with memories flashing through me as briefly as gunfire at night. The belief that things had shape and weight dissolved, and the idea of matter seemed merely a whim, concealing that all there was to existence was a disturbance of the relations between things which themselves did not exist. This sudden, passing awareness exploded beyond my imagination and destroyed it. I do not know how long it was before there began what proved to be only a halting and partial reconstruction of consciousness.

The first suffusion of new awareness was the fragrance of human skin. In a constant delight of steady sensation it re-created me as an ungraduated and eternal love; there seemed no other reality than the emotion of humanness. I felt like an animal back among its kind. Even when the contrasts of other human odours permeated the sweet fragrance of the skin, what by habit would have produced disgust now gave texture to pleasure. Staleness conveyed repose; foulness, strength; goatiness, a gaudy excitement. I began to scent this person and that, affectionate towards each, loving them all.

A child laughed and I was happy. The feeling of a

woman's song was sad, yet it gave me courage. I felt the warmth when humans reached out to touch each other's hands or hold each other's bodies; and pity when a girl cried. There was collective noise and movement. I felt the beating heart of a frightened enemy. A scowl excited challenges. Tears and cries for pity raised a lust for turmoil. Emotions contended, threat against threat. Laughter suggested the desire to turn it to tears. There was the terror of dying children; but the fear of those who had slaughtered them turned to love at the sight of children of their own.

I began to feel that I was in one special place. It was a high building. I could feel its height, its closeness to water, the materials of which it was made, its divisions, its little rooms and corridors, its big rooms and assembly places, set above each other, floor upon floor. Brought into it and spread throughout it was some large, particular group of people. I could feel all of their individual hopes and fears at once, a vast disorder of confidence and peril, like some enormous sum in arithmetic in which the positives and negatives interacted to give exactly nothing as the final answer.

But the building had some purpose. At first it seemed to be an arena in which those assembled were enacting two rival beliefs. By constantly spending their own hopes, as buoyant as prayers, one side seemed to pay tribute to an abundant optimism; the other side sustained the comforts of expected failure. I felt many times two contestants look at the same thing: one saw it bright, one saw it dark. It was as if the colours had been painted on their eyeballs, blinding them.

Then vanity seemed the purpose more likely to have brought these people together in the building. Some sought reflections of their excellence by displaying it, some by playing a small part in the displays of others; some vanities grew in contest; others in private admiration. I felt the blood beat as a man flexed his muscles, grimaced,

108

shouted boasts, stamped his feet and cupped his balls in his hand; yet with some other part of me I knew that this man was alone in a room, his self-love swelling in his own mind as he contemplated some new idea so intently that he reached for the head of his penis, to touch it through his clothing, admiring his cleverness.

Was the purpose of the building to test love and comradeship? Some of the people in it seemed to care most about seeking in each other a friendship that could survive whatever threats came to it in the building; others that they should at least find in an ironic companionship a quiet and dignified release from the insults that their life in common otherwise offered to them; some had a modest but strong desire to feel familiar and predictable to each other, even if unhappily; others found desire by looking at each other's bodies. At times I could feel a superior congratulate himself on his own goodness because he had treated an inferior as a member of the same species; at other times I sensed that an underling was congratulating himself for forgiving one of his masters an insult. Many of them best expressed their comradeship by taking a drug and moving towards their ideal of humanness by chemical means.

Yet the purpose of the building also seemed to be the glorification of conquest. I was conscious of one person whose blood jerked more quickly through his body when he sensed submission but blood sank from his skin when he in turn submitted to a larger strength. In another I could feel the prickling doubt of one who provoked attack because he hoped for defeat. There was another who sought to humble a greater strength than his own: I felt the sweat twist up through tiny ducts and burst across the dead cells of his palms. Two men were together, both their stomachs shrunken and dry. One was enraged, the other frightened. Nerves pulled their arteries tight, made their muscles stiffen and their breath come faster. I felt the blood in one of them flow back to his skin, and the wet excite-

109

ment of his stomach's churning: it was as if he were now eating the other.

For a time it seemed clear that the purpose of the building was to tend to the pride of one great personage. I felt him preen and peck as he capriciously disturbed the emotions of others, and then trembled with irritation at any attack on his own self-regard. His huge abysses of sorrow were deep enough to contain compassion for the degradations of the whole species, but they were melodramas of his own self-pity at the defeat of some minor vanity. It was as if he were attempting to digest and absorb everything in the building so that he alone could give himself perfect shape and colour: he alone was to seem great, and be capriciously free. When he exulted, the others were to exult; when he was afraid, they were to be afraid; when he was at peace, they were to be at peace; when he was restless, they were to be restless. Some of them seemed to have gutted themselves and stuffed their bodies with his substance. Either they made every one of their actions a tribute to his wisdom, waiting for his smiles, or they offered their defiance so that he could destroy it and lift them above their failures. When they contested with each other in their own vanities it was sometimes in their love for him, or his for them, that they contested. But did this great personage exist? Or had he been invented by some of those in the building because they needed him?

There was some other purpose to the building. There seemed to be a pulse in it, giving it rhythm, diastolic-systolic, expanding and contracting, good-bad, benign-malign. From one heartbeat to the next the same man could love the great personage of the building, then hate him, then love him again. As this sense of alternation grew stronger I recognised that there were two great men, not one, and that to some the dispute about which of the two was the true god, and which the false, was now the main purpose of the building.

110

Soon I began to be troubled by a range of emotions that were quite different and much less strong. These emotions appeared likely to provide the key to the building's purpose. Most of those in it seemed, however mildly, to want the building and the relations of the people in it to go on surviving. Their loyalty was to walls and floors, corridors and furniture, and great persons merely went with the place, like lifts or doors. It seemed possible that the building's main purpose was to cause most of those in it to go on doing the same things each day without enquiring why they did them.

Suddenly I was aware of the purpose that all the people in the building professed to give to their actions. Discussions of anything that affected the affairs of the building had to be conducted in terms of this official belief, and following it was so important that it could excuse the overriding of any other consideration, even honesty or kindness. For some there was a pleasant ruthlessness in this, good exercise, making the blood run faster, and with a finality about it, like shooting an enemy. For others it offered a nervous, boastful amusement. The deluded belief shared by all these people was that the only reason they had been brought together was to make a profit for the organisation that paid them and owned the building. Their other cravings could not be confessed directly, only in the terms of accountancy. This simple faith led them even to the absurdity of believing that they were all graduated in degrees of importance according to how far they could help the organisation to make more money.

CHAPTER 10

the lion

The sky was clogged with muddy clouds cracked like a parched river bed; the water of the bay polished the reflection of their drabness with a faint glistening of silver. Seagulls rocked with the swell, and a brilliant turquoise oil-slick undulated on the water. The seagulls screamed up into the air, drifted, then circled, wings beating strongly.

From the bay stretched a wide open passage of grey water, indented by all the other bays. I was looking out at the port of my native city, and I knew that beyond were the two stone headlands that sheltered it, and then the ocean. I felt a shudder of sentiment; we had marched through the streets of this city in our new uniforms and then sailed out between those headlands.

I knew that I was in the building which was the prison of all the hopes and fears that had been revealed to me, but I did not know what was going on in every part of it. Wide windows opened out on the bay and behind them was the emptiness of a conference room. A long table of dark wood stretched down its centre like a giant's coffin, mourned by heavy chairs in black leather which stood on a thick carpet of biscuit colour, only a few shades lighter than the paint on the walls. I seemed to be in a room that had been fashioned

112

out of dough and then baked.

Why was I here? Why, without a word, but with such love, had I lent myself so absolutely to the designs of the Prince? I began to compose some of the phrases in the arguments I might have raised, and the agreements I might have expressed, if, when the Prince had made his speeches, I had done something other than nod and smile. I sounded out a paragraph or two of the oration I might have put together and I phrased several subtle questions; I even began to imagine the promises that would have poured from me. But how could I have promised anything if I did not know what it was I was supposed to do? Why had he sent me? Why had I come? In memory I could see his arm stiffen, and again I felt my submission to a radiant and mighty purpose, but as this glow of submission faded I still saw the arm, flicked towards me. This was the characteristic gesture of the illusionist, maintained in all his disguises. Was the illusionist, when I first met him, merely a representation of the Prince in some other form? Or was the idea of the Prince so much in demand that, as with Santa Claus in department stores, many men were needed to play his part?

A young woman came into the conference room to lay out some notepaper and pencils, as if they were prayer books for a mourning. (It appeared that I was not in the room, at least not in the ordinary sense, for she could not see me.) When a young man came in and I felt, as with a hand, the softness and warmth between the woman's thighs, I knew that I was experiencing some of his emotions. This occupied me for only a few seconds; when I lost it and was again aware of the room's colour and shape he was not, as I had imagined, fondling her but shyly wishing her good-morning and making the best of it when, still putting out notebooks and pencils, she did not look up.

Other men arrived and began a meeting. My senses and emotions flickered so rapidly that I was shocked into incomprehension. Some sense of concentration returned, but it was the earlier and wider and more confusing awareness; again it was the whole building that I comprehended, with the same uncertainties.

The central preoccupation of the building now seemed to be someone known as The Woman. I saw her lips, under me, parted. Her eyes, dark with grease, glanced at me from long, stiff lashes. Spread out, her hair glowed in the sun, but it did not move; only its colour flashed and changed. I felt her cheek against mine, quiet and still; her long cool fingers touched me, indifferent. I felt the hairless childishness of her genitals, and the plug inside. At times her parts seemed to be lying on a surgeon's table, cut into pieces—a pale severed hand, neatly curled; a scalp, flayed from the skull, sterilised, and spread out like a butterfly's wings; lips mounted on plastic.

I heard one group discussing these lips. It was as if they had formed in a queue to suck and lick eternal life out of them, yet there was no thrust of passion about it, unless it was that the only lips The Woman would kiss were her own. Another group talked about her breasts, not of nipples springing up at the touch and stirring the body, but of a kind of mask of the breasts, encasing The Woman's real breasts so that they lay flaccid and without feeling behind it. Those who talked of her odour hated it, smothering it with liquids of their own intricate recipe; those who praised her hair also hated it, except on the scalp, and then only if it were some colour other than her own. A whole group wished her legs to achieve some form so perfect that The Woman herself could love them; apparently she was to spend a significant part of the day stooped in self-admiration.

It had now become obvious that the building served its faith in money by designing and selling things to women —cosmetics to rub on their faces, dyes with which to drench their hair, ointments to smear on their skins, chemicals to inhibit the odours of their decomposition, garments to

114

change the shape of their breasts or the central parts of their bodies, plugs to block their menstrual juices. The Woman was not any particular human—no such person could exist—but a hypothesis that helped those in the building to get on with their work.

I was again aware of the conference room. The men at the meeting had begun to discuss what they described as marketing plans and it was at once clear that they were putting into these schemes more comprehensive staff work than had gone into our disastrous landing on the beach. There even seemed to be a greater sense of an enemy. For us our enemies were an unknown people with whom we were to share an adventure. For these men, as they spoke the language of military calculation, with "woman" instead of "the enemy" and "sell" instead of "kill", there was an anticipation of personal triumph.

Two of them left the room, called briefly to some other and apparently more important meeting. With these two gone, the others became as lively as little boys. They gossiped about the rivalry between the two great personages who were contesting for control of all that happened in the building. They were all supporters of the younger of the two, speaking of him as "the chief", although one of them, more cautious than the others, spoke of him as "the chief executive". The older contestant was referred to more formally as "the governing director" or, ironically, "the gov.", but even when his full title was given it was spoken with a slight derision, as if, despite his title, he governed nothing. Only when one of them mentioned "the gov." by name did I understand that the president of the follies of this building was my oldest friend, the comrade of the trenches whose name I had given as the first I wished to see on my journey.

I had last seen him in our dusty trench when I answered the enemy's challenge. He was then half risen from our game of cards, as if about to pull me back. In the darkest period of my time on the beaches I had wondered whether he had really risen to save me or whether he was feinting. Perhaps I had jumped up in an attempt at last to match his own hot bravery, which he carried on so intently that to most of us it was a kind of social embarrassment.

Even when we were children he had acted with abstracted and lonely concentration, apparently imagining that he was leading us when he was not. He would see nothing but what he was next determined to do. He would become so grave-faced about it that often he would not notice the rest of us until his pride was affronted by failure. He might then act so spitefully that I would have knocked him down, had our friendship not demanded that I should fight the others.

In my time of questioning, when I wondered bitterly if friendship was anything more than habit or, at best, knowledge, I could at first find no memory of love for my companion; all that I missed in his absence was familiarity, and all that I seemed to love was my knowledge of him, which at first seemed small, since most of our companionship had concerned itself not with what we were but with forgetting ourselves in recklessness. And then, along with so many other miseries, as I thought of him, I yearned for him. In at last sensing the emptiness and the fragility that inspired his courage, I knew something of at least one other human.

His arrogance made him so fidgety that if he came to one of the dinners I sometimes arranged when we were students he might say nothing, silent until we left the restaurant and the two of us were walking through the city streets back to the rooms we rented in an old house near the water. Out of his memories of the conversation he would then snatch some freak remark and from it construct a stratagem of his own. He might talk until dawn, expanding his outlandish idea with a vehemence of imagination which would not have been surprising in some visionary but which was always ingeniously connected to some small

116

practical matter, if usually with such little chance of success that perhaps it was visionary after all.

I was more of the world than he was, and more capable of reasoning, but I had expected that if he did not sacrifice himself altogether to his boldness he might later lend it to some great cause and rise above us. Now he seemed to have used his life neither in boldness nor for a cause. He seemed merely to have mislaid it.

In the foreign city where we gathered before embarking on our expedition, four of us went with him to a brothel. We stretched out in five cubicles, side by side, their thin walls not reaching the ceiling. For fear of pickpockets we put our tunics under the beds and kept the rest of our uniforms on, even the boots, merely hitching up our shirts and pulling down our breeches. The beds heaved and squeaked; as we performed our acts into them the prostitutes shouted to each other in their own language and we began shouting to each other in ours. When it was over and we were drinking wine and laughed about our exploit, my companion said: "That's the way it should always be done." Several days later, on the morning of our landing, he was ablaze with boldness; on one occasion he forced our officer to lead us so far ahead of the other groups that, although we held our ground for a while, we were called back: only he and I survived the retreat. What had he learned about women since then? Or was this building of vanities also a kind of brothel that could be controlled only by a man?

I began listening again to the men in the conference room. After their first liveliness, which proved nothing more than a celebration that two enemies had left, they had become listless: they were talking as hard as ever, but drily, like men repeating a conversation to reassure themselves of their own rightness. They were retelling anecdotes which justified their view of my comrade as an ignorant blunderer and of themselves as clever men who were rightly coming into their own. From this I was able to understand the

117

history of my friend's fortunes and misfortunes. The complex of business companies at present in the building had been assembled by him. He had built up a company of his own, had bought other companies with borrowed money, had secured control over others by merger, and then, to round off his collection (and to make an enormous profit), he had sold the lot to a foreign company which had left him with the highest position in the building, on the understanding that he would no longer exercise power. He was to have left all of his power to the foreigner who had been made the chief executive, but he had recently taken advantage of a drop in company sales to break this agreement.

According to one of the men in the conference room, my old comrade was like a drunken sailor, buying anything he saw and then waking up in the morning and pawning it all to get some cash. Each of the men spoke of him as if he were a lucky idiot: even the profitability of the companies when he had controlled them was taken as merely an example of his short-sightedness, and the fact that he had criticised the chief executive's policies because they had been accompanied by a fall in sales was just another example of the ignorance and impatience that prevented him from taking what they called a broad view.

They became sentimental about him. He had been a great man in his day. His main fault was to have clung too long to power, into an age whose customs he did not comprehend any more than he understood the latest whims of the women who bought the things his companies made. They scorned his desire to gain an honour from the government, and told anecdotes about how he had tried to earn it by serving on several senseless committees. In this part of the conversation their main complaint against him seemed to be that he was no longer in vogue.

Others came into the room. My friend had unexpectedly called a meeting, and would be in the conference room in a few minutes. While some quickly left and others hurried in to take their places, I thought of his sharp young face, eagerly pushing towards adventure, grave and expectant. He would sit like a man about to leap, yet he could leave a room so gracefully and quietly that you did not notice he had gone. He was proud of his body's slimness and springiness, showing it off as if it were an animal he had trained to do tricks.

A short, fat old man came into the room. Everyone stood up. It was my friend. He sat at the head of the table and, one arm akimbo, began to read a document. Everyone sat down. He was as blown-up as a dead cow; his buttocks and thighs were so gross that he leant forward in his chair to relieve himself of their weight, his swollen belly pressing against the table as if in all this blubber to find some hardness. Rage creased his eyes, blood flushed his cheeks. From one side of his lips there was a faint sizzle of spit and an occasional slurp, which he would check with his hand. Fat fingers stroked a hairless scalp, or a badge in the lapel of his jacket. When he had finished reading the document he threw it in front of him and said: "The answer is no."

Arguments were now being put up for him to knock down. Charts had been prepared, but he waved them away. Written reports were offered, but he refused to read them, insisting on one occasion that he should be told about a document of a hundred or so pages in two minutes. Several of those who had intended to submit reports for his approval took them off the table and put them on their laps, like table napkins. One of these reports he demanded to see; he read it through quickly and praised it, insisting that the only good reports ever prepared in the building were those that people were not brave enough to show him. When someone put a hidden report back on the table, he said he had no further time for reports, he had a general statement to make, and it would be as well if everyone took notes since it represented the company's policy for the year. He began dictating what he described as general marketing

119

approaches. Since all of the documents, reports and charts were also concerned with this purpose, he seemed to have swept away all the work that had been done in the building and replaced it with a few impromptu remarks of his own. As he went on, he consulted some notes, stumbling here and there in his delivery as if the notes had been written by someone else. When he had finished he said he did not want any further discussion of the matter. He was outlining the board's general policy. It was unfortunate that the chief executive was away sick (how was he, by the way?) but he would, of course, be informed of these decisions when he returned. Now, since it was almost lunchtime, he would like everyone to have a drink. He remained seated while others stood around the bar (which had been hidden behind folding doors). He called people to him, teased them briefly, as if they were puppies, and then sent them off, calling for others.

I could feel all the admiration and resentment his intervention had caused, the frustrated anger at his stupidity, the respect for his wisdom, the fear for his unexpected defiance of the chief executive, the admiration for its boldness, the perplexity as to what he had been talking about and how its ambiguities could be translated into action, the sense of tedium that so much work had been wasted and that so much more work would now have to be done to make sense of his jottings, the excitement that things were changing. Unexpectedly, I could feel the sweat on the soles of his feet. As he sat there, delighted in his capriciousness, the blood squirted out of his heart at high speed. He was afraid of his own boldness, and delighted by his fear as by a drug his body needed to relieve it of boredom.

He dismissed them all except one, who sat down beside him. A waitress came in and they ordered lunch. His companion reported to him on a meeting the chief executive (who was recovering from influenza) had called at his house at eight o'clock that morning. He described the instructions the chief executive had issued (which were quite the opposite to my comrade's) and the comments various officials had made upon them. He told how, in the line of *his* new marketing philosophy, the chief executive was refurnishing his house, selling off his antiques and replacing them with furniture of more modern style because he considered that the general impression people had of the company (which he called its "image") must no longer be that of a traditional and prestigious firm but of an up-and-coming newcomer. "Well," said my friend, "after what I've told them this morning he'll have to buy his antiques back again."

His lunchtime companion was the author of the notes he had read to the meeting as the board's policy. My friend now saw it as *his* policy. He began to talk of the board meeting he had summoned for that evening in order to emphasise its importance, and of how he would get the board to acquiesce in the policy he had already attributed to them. He boasted of how he had spent the earlier part of the morning dismissing a number of the company's oldest employees because at the board's last meeting the chief executive had said that there should be stability in the company's staffing policy and this statement had been criticised by some of the board members. "I'll bring that up first," he said. "I've got him there." On the other hand, on the matter of a strike in a factory that manufactured some of the products about which the people in the building found so much occasion for dispute, he was considering making some criticism of the chief executive's intransigence. He had already issued instructions for a settlement favourable to the strikers. As he recounted his defiance his muscles relaxed. He said that after lunch he would sleep for a while in his office. On his way out of the conference room he announced that at the board meeting he would appeal to his compatriots' pride in their country and urge them not to leave their company's affairs in the hands of a foreigner.

The waitress came in and removed the plates. It was still overcast outside.

"We are quite familiar with the parallels between what you have witnessed and the conduct of medieval barons, and so forth. We are also familiar with all the other political parallels as between one stage of history and the other. Please don't bother to make any of these obvious comparisons."

I was abased with the pain of the computer's sudden intervention. All my senses had again dissolved, except that of hearing, if this *was* hearing. But although not ready for the sensation, I tried to speak for myself and ask questions about my mission. Fighting through the pain this caused, I tried to break the stubbornness of the computer with my own will. The computer was silent, and I was not sure what to do. My thoughts seemed to turn in on me, like a deafening and meaningless echo.

"The period in this experiment in which you are required to communicate, though in an elementary way, has now arrived," said the computer. "By not co-operating you are merely delaying the test. You may agree or disagree with what I say, or even not be interested in it, but please do not interrupt. I was simply, as you would put it, saying the first thing that came into my head. I could have conjugated French irregular verbs or counted up to a hundred to test the clarity of communication, but I have chosen instead to give you some of my views on a matter on which you are probably not yet fully informed. Now think silence. I speak, then I tell you when to speak. When you have finished, you again think silence. We shall now recite the first four lines of 'Mary had a little lamb'. I shall begin. Think silence." The computer recited the nursery rhyme to me several times. Whenever I thought of something other than silence my thoughts rebounded back at me in echo. When the recitation was finished I still thought silence, to allow the computer to give me its next instructions. There was no reaction. I continued to think of silence.

Slowly, the other parts of my consciousness were restored.

Masses of cloud floated across a sky that was now pale blue. The dark green of the bay was flecked black with ripples, and the blue-black of the main harbour was chopped white. The scene was anxious and inhospitable, self-concerned, not the welcoming calm of deep blue water and sky of my memory.

From the top floor of the building, looking farther out across the harbour than anyone could have seen when I lived in this city, I saw that the olive green of the trees that had lined so many of the bays was replaced with concrete or brick, although at the water's edge the sandstone remained. The tall, pale buildings, drifting anonymously in the air, fulfilled the prophecies of the old novels of fantasy, yet the city did not seem unfamiliar; it had merely changed its clothes.

In the anteroom to the suite from which my old friend administered the vehicles of self-importance his two secretaries were leaning on their typewriters, gossiping with a young man about my friend's unpredictabilities, his forgetfulness, his unexpected generosities and his sense of excitement. He amused them like an ambitious child always reaching out for novelty and therefore sometimes naughtily touching the wrong thing. There was no one in my friend's room. His desk, as big as the floor of a small room, was covered at its ends with neat stacks of letters, memoranda and reports; at its centre where, as at a child's sandtray, he grappled with affairs, papers lay in a kind of rubbish heap. The desk and some of the furniture immediately around it were of the period I remembered, suggesting that he had tried to keep something of his younger self near him; otherwise his room was as anonymous as his secretaries'. Here, in something that seemed more crypt than room, my friend would sit at the altar end, surrounded by his familiar possessions, but already an alien. When he died, or when he went, his things could simply be bundled away and the room would claim its next inhabitant. Among the litter of photographs on a bookcase behind his desk, I saw one of him as I had known him, posing in his field service dress, slim and ready for a fight. Among the medals pinned to his tunic, I was not surprised to see our country's highest military award.

At one end of the office, beyond an open door, was a room furnished in the same style as the conference room of the morning's meeting, but not as large, except for its bar, which seemed twice as big. The door at its farther end was locked. In the sitting-room behind it my friend lay asleep on a couch. The creases of anger on his face had relaxed; he looked as peaceful as one calmly pondering some new aspect of reality. The slow rhythm of his brain leapt into nothingness. There was the flicker of a dream, a mere blank flash of consciousness, then again only the gentle undulations of life without memory.

A key turned in the door. A woman came in. She sat in a chair, smoked part of a cigarette and looked at him. I could feel the faint but steady pulsations of his brain and the disorder of hers as she scanned him with contempt, then with a certain sense of familiarity, as if he were a household task. Within the familiarity there was some softness, a slight reaching-out towards him, but this hardened into anger, and with the anger there came some excitement of sexual desire, faint, but sharpening as she began to undress.

Naked, she sat in the chair again, still smoking, and fondled her nipples as if to prepare herself for his embraces, shutting and opening her eyes. The anger of what she saw increased her excitement. When she stretched herself out

124

beside him she smiled, made as if to crush her cigarette on his arm, put it in the ashtray instead, and for a while lay still, her eyes closed, her mouth open, her hands on her breasts. When she woke him, she did it with a couple of bites, given gently, but with enough hatred to further sharpen her excitement. By now she seemed eager for pleasure. Anger returned to his face, and when he was fully awake he embraced her so quickly and roughly that she shuddered. As in a rehearsed game, she made to scratch his back with her fingernails. He seized her hands and fought with her, attempting to spreadeagle her while she mimed resistance. Excited by her pretences, he mounted her while she still struggled.

As he began to perform his act they both again shut their eyes, but as his desire rose, hers ran less hot; she had stopped struggling, simulating instead the heaves and gasps of passion. I felt in her mind the sensation of one who gives orders—*thighs, strain! mouth, pant!*—as if she were the captain of a ship and the members of her body its crew. Desire pulsated a little when she put up in her mind, one by one, a series of *tableaux vivants* of erotic postures in which she was the only participant; but she did not find what she was looking for. The ship of which she was the commander sailed on in darkness, its ropes creaking and its sails cracking according to order but with its captain now contemplating what she would do after dinner.

As my friend's brief frenzy approached its climax he was thinking of strong naked young men with whom he was at the same time fighting and performing sexual acts of a complexity that had never entered my imagination. His interest concentrated on one of them. It was his memory of me, still clear to him after so long. In his mind he was tearing my balls off. At this moment his excitement reached its crisis and its conclusion.

I had seen his fat old body push itself into this enactment of lust and I had seen his mind reach for the old pieces of rubbish in it so that his limbs could sustain the role he still demanded of them; yet, although what had happened was so removed from our ideals of such occasions, his climax had nevertheless a sweetness and innocence, and while his partner was hastily and convincingly accompanying him by miming a passion she did not feel, the sensation of his pleasure was no different from what it would have been if he were still a smooth-cheeked youth, thrusting with strong young limbs. As he lay there for a while, quite still, he was beyond age and beyond comparison, part of the human fragrance.

When he rolled off her and lay on his back, his eyes still shut, desire seemed to return to his partner, but when she made some gestures of lust he pushed her aside and went into the bathroom. While he was away she made love to herself, quickly, and then began to dress. He was confident and bumptious when he came back, speaking to her happily, as to a trusted friend, of what he intended to do at tonight's board meeting. He told her jokes, unexpectedly seeking her affection, skilfully coaxing her into smiles. They resembled two rogues, laughing over their rogueries, teasing each other with a play of what could not be done seriously. When she got up he gave her some money and, reaching into a drawer, took out several handfuls of cosmetics and pushed them into her handbag. She kissed him for reward and waved to him with friendship as she left by the private door.

Some of the directors were already in the board room when my friend arrived. Among them was the chief executive. He sat apart, reading documents and making notes. My friend walked over and shook his rival's hand, congratulating him on this unexpectedly quick recovery from his sickness. In the chief executive I sensed the same challenge of intelligent resolution that the Prince had shown, but he seemed to prefer to appear a man of great care and prudence.

Perhaps before he had openly contested for power the Prince had also known how to lower his eyes.

The chief executive was speaking to two of the directors about ways of cheating women into buying one grease for their skins rather than another, discussing this with the meticulousness of one planning the prosecution of some great cause; then, with the softness of a seducer, he talked of what he called his "marketing philosophy", as if perhaps, after all, he was concerned not so much with selling rubbish to women as with insisting that events should have a certain pattern and that he should appear to be a certain kind of person. The contrast between the gravity of his manner and the childish occasion of it matched the contrast between his outward caution and the urges I could feel beating within him. As he moved past a window, standing for a moment against the darkness of the night, he again seemed so like the Prince that I wondered why the others had not felt his power. It was apparently more in the outward roughness of my comrade that they saw strength, although some of them seemed to distrust it.

When the meeting started they all began fighting about its purpose. Their emotions rushed and rebounded, taking direction not so much from initial impetus as from what they hit. For a time they seemed like carnival balloons with faces painted on them, floating up and then shrivelling to a wrinkled flabbiness. My friend had gained some initiative, shooting forward angrily in attack, causing turmoil and riding over it, making whatever arguments suited his purpose; but now he was heaving in his chair like a winded animal. The others were listening to a long speech from the chief executive. Having boldly advanced behind the steady shield of reason, he began to attack with slow strokes. One of the directors broke in, but the chief executive knew how to let his opponents reveal their excesses.

Most of the directors talked loudly without declaring for either my comrade or the chief executive. One of them asked for a pause in the meeting. He wanted to draft a statement; his speech suggested that the statement would leave my comrade again powerless. Another director supported him. There was a break for coffee and sandwiches while the two of them went into another room. One of my comrade's associates sat at a small table drafting a statement of his own.

With the coffee there was an attempt at amiability among those who seemed least committed. My old comrade went off into his office with two of his supporters and when he came back and called the meeting together he brushed away both of the drafted statements, producing instead a document of his own, which was, he said, a motion of no confidence in the chief executive, signed by two directors. He at once shone with sympathetic kindness. He spoke softly and wisely, suggesting that, to avoid embarrassment, there be no formal vote; instead he would ask for an informal expression of opinion. It was a matter of great distress to him, he said, that the companies he and his board had built up, and of which he was the governing director, should become the subject of so much discord. His only concern was their continued prosperity—he was sure that the same went for all of them—and, despite his friendship with the chief executive, a man of great ability, he thought that if the meeting showed its lack of confidence, the interests of their common enterprise demanded the chief executive's resignation. The present foreign owners of the company would, of course, be asked to agree to this change. My comrade said that despite his many other commitments, he was ready to fly to the city where the owners had their headquarters and settle the matter with them himself. He concluded with a few general remarks, expressed in the benign confidence of a commander who, having recaptured the initiative, now offered clemency.

The chief executive spoke briefly, with no passion except the weariness of a wise parent who can foresee each

128

of a child's follies. He introduced a letter from the foreign owners and read it aloud. After praising his past record, it went on to say that he had been appointed a director of the parent company and was therefore one of the most honoured governors in its international enterprise. Several ambiguous phrases seemed to express in advance a lack of interest in whatever my comrade and his associates might care to do; other phrases seemed to suggest new titles for them, international travel, and other inducements.

My old comrade announced that he'd had enough and unless the chief executive went he would resign. What's more, he'd publish the reason for his resignation, and would denounce the company's foreign ownership publicly and continuously. He had fought for his country in two wars; he believed that his country was the best in the world, and he would consider it his duty not to end his days as a puppet controlled from a foreign city. He called on the board to summon its love for its country and join him in offering to resign: by making this threat they would serve the interests of the company's many faithful employees; the foreign company would be unlikely to risk such public dispute. He had already discussed these matters with his many powerful friends in the political party that governed the country and he was assured of their support.

Three directors immediately pledged their resignations. No one else spoke. Someone moved that the meeting be adjourned. The next day was a public holiday, so perhaps they could meet again on the day after it. Most of the directors left the room quickly. Their cars shot out of the basement, tyres squealing, into dark, empty streets.

My old comrade stayed on in the board room with the three who had declared their support of him. They sat drinking whisky, and as they drank, their rage and confidence increased. The three congratulated my friend again and again on his boldness and they began making lists of which members of the board each of them would lobby.

129

They put through phone calls, discussing plans with others, and fabricating a scheme to buy back the company, or parts of it, making lists of supporters they might look to for this purpose. Each of them boasted of the politicians who owed him something, of the men he could threaten, of the newspaper support he could expect, of the guile he would use with this one and the flattery with that.

Again convinced of their importance and cunning, they began to talk about some minor war in which one of their sons was at present engaged, and then of the wars they themselves had fought in. My old comrade, alone of them, had been present at our landing on the beach. Its anniversary was to be celebrated the next day and as he talked about it they listened with the modesty of those who recognise that they have missed their country's greatest occasion. When he had finished, they paused for a while so as not to appear to be capping his story.

Their drunkenness made me excited and sure, surrounded by brothers in a simple world, just as I had felt when, in a night as dark as this one, the ships of our expedition had come to rest off a foreign coast.

It was a different computer that now seized my consciousness, but with equal pain. It explained that this particular form of communication was its special field of research and that to avoid a second fiasco it would supervise communication with me itself. The previous computer had specialised in studying humans and did not seem equipped for more precise work. "In this stage of experiment," it said, "you must attempt to communicate with me. If this proves successful, the next stage might be to hold a test dialogue about something or other. When you attempt your communication, think your thoughts as sentences. Do not try to divulge your whole mind. It is not possible, and even if it were we would not know what to make of it. For several hundred years some of your species have been trying to be natural, free, to express themselves. What can they do? Wiggle their bodies around unconventionally? Jabber? Wear their hair differently? Put things upside-down? You cannot convert your minds into outward metaphors. You cannot *express yourselves*. You can only *be yourselves,* and in that you have little choice. Speak to me grammatically, and as logically as you can. By doing so you confine what you are saying. But this is the only way you can say anything. By this means we have a convention in which one thing can be spoken of in terms of another. There is no finality about it, except that it may finally be nonsense, but at least it seems to be useful in keeping things going, and there are rules to the game."

I asked if I was to report on my impressions.

"In this second stage," said the computer, "just talk for a while, about anything, as a kind of practice conversation. Our immediate instructions are only to open channels of communication with you. Presumably they will be used to some purpose later in your mission."

I began to form sentences. All awareness of the computer vanished. I concentrated on my own words. I may as well have been reading out a street directory. I was aware of the computer again. It told me to think sentences about something that interested me. This would help my concentration.

I said to myself, and presumably to the computer, that, although he was enmeshed in trivialities, and, in his obsessions, was indifferent to the methods he used or the results to others of what he did, I could feel in my old comrade the excitements, the attempts to find freedom in decision, the cravings for the unexpected that I had learned to recognise as the promptings of a hero. In his anger and pride he was displaying the desire to protect his honour. In more solemn circumstances his recklessness might have been praised. Remembering the computer's instructions, I then thought silence.

131

"In themselves, the sentences are communicating quite clearly," said the computer. "Think some more, this time at somewhat greater length."

I said that if heroism was to have meaning as a style, its recognition must surely not depend only on circumstance. Since the heroic style could be recognised not only on great occasions but on trivial ones, there should also perhaps be a morality of heroism, related to the occasion, so that one could speak of a good hero or a bad one, or, as in my friend's case, of an irrelevant one. The end of heroism, its test, was often violence, and it was of interest to my central point—and one on which the Prince had declared himself—that one could, of course, speak of a morality of violence. If this were not possible one could never speak of the history of humanity except with loathing, and even if to do so were one's mode there would at least be degrees of loathing.

Realising that I had not yet spoken long enough for the purpose of the test, I added that those who were taken up simply by one style or the other—the boldness of my friend's style or the affected caution of the chief executive's (itself another kind of boldness) —were not necessarily by that choice (if that was the word) either right or wrong. This would depend on the occasion. If heroism could be good or bad, then so could prudence. There were heroic times when the excesses of rashness made caution and calculation seem more highly prized, and there were prudent times when out of boredom, or even to face danger, men longed for heroism. Just as it was pointless to dispute on the side of one or the other as to its practical effects, both heroism and prudence could also be equally right or wrong as ways of looking at the world. To the calculating, heroism could seem merely selfish romanticism, but then reason and pragmatism were romantic too, and often provided a wilfully misleading guide to events. Events were so difficult to comprehend that thinking about them did not necessarily lead to an understanding of them: what it could do was to ennoble circumstances and release energies for action. Yet one need not despair. To follow the style of reason could enlarge dreams of what might be; to follow the style of a hero could equally enlarge human ambition; in either case, by following a style persistently, one could give to one's own life, and perhaps to the lives of others, some special interest before one died. Perhaps those who most gained in both experience and imagination were those who, although in conflict with themselves, were caught up in both the style of the lion and the style of the fox. As to whether they were also touched by goodness—that was another matter. I thought silence until the computer came in. "This time," it said, "think something quite short."

I said that obviously my friend was seeking a true hero's end to his career by engaging in metaphors of victory and defeat. If he failed to save his honour by winning he would save it by the protests and excitements of losing, which to him would still be victory.

"Say something else now," said the computer. "Do not limit it to any length. Keep on thinking sentences until you feel me stopping you. This is the second part of the test."

It had occurred to me, I said, that if my friend resigned he might, although his motives were those of personal honour, turn them to some matter of public pride. Patriotism, since he might be forced into it, could well serve this purpose. Perhaps this was how history worked: that men, in their struggles with each other, found causes and that the causes were whatever happened to be lying around. They quarrelled over the great banquet of power, and then, to lend dignity to their squabble, strode into the guardroom to pick up whatever banners were lying against the wall. If one of the issues of the day in my country was foreign ownership then my old comrade, having wasted so much of his heroism on matters of no importance, might, if he lived a little longer, lend his heroism to a more serious theme and even again snatch at the fame that was one of the consolations among the disasters of heroism. That he could do it gracefully, however, now seemed beyond belief. Of course, if it proved that he had chosen an unpopular cause he would merely make a fool of himself, and if he had chosen a cause that would grow, but not in his lifetime, he would never know if his greatness would later be recognised. I felt the thud of the computer's will. I thought silence.

"I shall now speak to you," said the computer. "At some stage I want you to interrupt me. I shall make no comment on your own observations. They do not interest me. I shall recite some mathematical tables, since that is something I know about. At some stage you must interrupt me with a question."

After the computer had recited a number of mathematical tables I willed it into silence, then asked if there was any indication yet as to the purpose of my mission. The computer said that its function was purely technical. It believed that a more sophisticated form of communication might be attempted next time. "I have tested some of the others," it said, "and you have done better than most of them. This test is now at an end." I tried to ask it who the others were, but there was no answer.

Although my session with the computer had seemed short, it was mid-morning before I was again aware of the city. I had the sensation of being in one of its streets. The traffic had stopped. Deserted buildings pointed towards a bland sky. At the end of certain empty streets I could see the backs of a crowd and beyond them, above their heads, banners carried in procession. A light wind blew towards me the faint sound of marching tunes and a scatter of cheers. I could imagine the long procession extending itself through the innards of the city as determinedly as a threat.

134

I remembered that this was the annual holiday that celebrated our landing on the beach.

In the streets through which the procession passed, most of the crowd contemplated the marching men in silence, as if they were a row of famous buildings. But the children cheered for their own excitement, and now and again some of their parents clapped. The procession extended up and down the street, filling it out, coming from somewhere, its head somewhere, its tail somewhere, its long body coiled through the city's main thoroughfares. I could see why the crowd was so silent. In watching the procession it was watching itself. The marchers had on their ordinary street clothes; nothing distinguished them from the onlookers except the common rhythm of their tread. Onlookers and marchers might have been interchanged without making any difference; who would fight and who would stand and clap was a matter of chance.

Each group of marchers bore in front of it a banner listing the military units its members had fought in, and sometimes the names of battles, thereby parading some of the century's follies. When the group consisting of my surviving old comrades came past, it was only by reading the banner in front of them that I knew who they were. They were so old, there were so few of them, they passed so quickly, that I recognised no one. The onlookers, also learning who they were from their banner, gave them a general cheer for being the only survivors of the occasion the day was celebrating. Behind them came the long ranks of those who had fought in later campaigns, or later wars, so that the rest of us from the earlier campaign were being represented by a system of continuing proxy. As the procession continued, the faces of the marchers became younger, and at its rear were men as young as my comrades had once been, springy-footed, their faces still in bloom, returned from some present war, grandsons or great-grandsons of those who led the march.

Into the office of my old comrade there came from outside the faint sound of a bagpipe's lament. The procession was over, but some of its bands were still playing here and there and thousands of former warriors were walking around as if they had seized the city, grouped in old companionships, their medals pinned to their jackets. Formed in a circle, a pipe band was playing for its own satisfaction in a park. Men sat in clusters on the grass and smoked. In the harbour, yachts cut through the water, celebrating a holiday.

My friend lay back in his chair, giving orders to those around him, leaned forward to scribble ideas on a pad or to telephone others to come into the office, and then leant back again. His jacket was off, thrown on a couch, the medals pinned to it shining in the light of a small lamp, and he was drinking whisky. It was as if he had shed some other self so that, unencumbered by memory, he could better engage in the depravities of his present office. All I could understand at first was that some new crisis had developed in the affairs of his firm and that those who had been summoned to the office were anxious to show pleasure at having been unexpectedly called to work on a holiday. Looking at the clock on the wall, I realised that this was the anniversary of that very hour when we were preparing to retreat from the hopeless position his rashness had forced us into. We had sweated into our uniforms as we lay behind some boulders, glancing back at the furze and dirt over which we were to escape, gripped by the fear that in a few moments bullets would tear our flesh apart.

From what he said into the telephone I learned that he had by accident, at a chance meeting with some government official several hours before, when the marchers were assembling, discovered (or created, I am not sure which) his firm's latest crisis. Although he spent a long time explaining that the chief executive had taken some wrong action, which he would now correct, and in congratulating himself on his own efficiency and courage, I still did not learn what the disturbance was about. A military band was now parading. Its leader's baton twisted, drumsticks flew in the air, feet stamped, and my excitement quickened.

Eventually I gathered that a filmed advertisement for a brand of women's brassiere manufactured by my comrade's firm had been banned by a board of censors, and that this was the crisis. Without telling my friend, the chief executive had agreed to change the advertisement. My comrade saw this as one of the dangers of foreign ownership —that it would pay any price to conciliate itself with a domestic government. In some way that was not clear to me, he was determined to make the censors change their ruling, thereby further exposing the chief executive's incompetence. He boasted of his friends in the government, sometimes as if a soft word from him would bring them running, sometimes as if he would threaten to resign from the government committees on which he served and reveal all that he knew about their absurdities and inefficiencies. As he drank more whisky he became more incoherent, railing against the government as well as foreign ownership. At one point he declared his patriotism by pointing to his medals and shouting that brave boys had not fought for their fucking country just so that a lot of foreign poofters could bugger them about. At another he expressed his concern for the freedom of the individual by shouting that the government could shove its fucking honours up its bum and that he didn't know what the country was coming to if a girl couldn't wiggle her fucking tits in a television advertisement. The others had become silent. They were waiting for the representatives of an advertising agency to arrive with a copy of the censored advertisement which opportunity had made my comrade so ready to defend that he had done so without seeing it. Outside, a small detachment of old soldiers marched by, led by four men carrying wreaths.

When three representatives of the advertising agency arrived, everyone went into a conference room, where the advertisement was at once projected on to a white screen. It was so short, no more than thirty seconds, and of such inanity that I could not at first understand what it was about. While a woman's voice spoke some triviality in a tone suggesting sexual desire, several other women, stripped to their undergarments, froze into unlikely poses, each pose held very briefly before another replaced it. So far as I could discover, it was not the poses that the censor had objected to but the fact that in one of them a breast encased in a brassiere had given a kind of quiver, as fleeting as a wink. Like an obsessive dream, the film was replayed many times while the men watching it sat is if drugged and sharing a common hallucination. Outside, a squad of uniformed young soldiers swung by, leading a long line of old men.

Throughout the repetitions of the film, and again back in my friend's office, two of the three agency representatives remained as silent as they could, as if the film had happened without their contrivance. These two were young, and brusque in manner. The third, an older man with anxious eyes and a nervy posture suggesting that age had brought him no wisdom, spoke boldly enough, in a quick delivery, but each time he replied to a challenge no one seemed to notice him; intent on their own conversation, the others cut across his boldness so that he did not finish what he had to say. Despite his age, he seemed subordinate to the two young men, and although, after my friend, he was the oldest in the room, he seemed the least significant.

Outside, a drunken marcher, his shabby suit rumpled, lifted a bugle to his lips and blew the Charge. The bystanders laughed at him, perhaps not knowing what it was he was blowing. Despite his drunkenness, the notes came through clearly and with command, as if we were about to set spur to our mounts and gallop across an unknown valley, our swords flashing and our spirits high. Inside, my friend was completing his instructions. He had arranged a meeting with the censors next day, summoning to it lawyers, advertising men, and his own followers. The bugler's notes seemed to punctuate his optimism as he planned telephone calls and private discussions, brassy and confident. But when the unknown bugler blew the Retreat, as if our charge had failed and the survivors were picking their way home through the corpses, my friend's continued high hope for the expression of his chicanery seemed already to be mocked by the chance of failure. He lifted the telephone, winking as he did it, and scratching his armpit. My attention was now with the advertising men, who were leaving. By a chance repetition of his name, I had learned that the eldest, and apparently the least significant of them, was my son.

the fox

When I was in the beach community I had at first felt some unease at knowing from the computers that I had a son aged fifty while I thought of myself as a man aged twenty-three. Then it occurred to me that some men measured time in the ageing of their children rather than in themselves, so that finally their children seemed emptied of love, not understanding the youthful aspirations of their parents. In this way I submerged all thought of this fifty-year-old man, my son. In my imagination I even attended his funeral, standing on the brittle yellow grass in a country cemetery while the cicadas drummed in the trees and the crows flapped against a hot wind. As the earth was shovelled onto the coffin and the dust rose I was aware that his mother was beside me. She was still in her youth, the only moist, fresh thing in this dryness, and in one of the freedoms of fantasy, no sooner was all the earth piled back into the grave than we set to among the wreaths, crushing and scattering the flowers that commemorated this stranger.

I had continued to re-enact in my mind the circumstances of her seduction, if that is the word for it: the warmth of her cheeks as I brushed them with my fingers in a gesture designed to be interpreted however she chose;

the suddenness with which she slipped the side of my hand into her mouth, caressing it with her tongue, then biting it; our embrace, our kisses; the softness of her body as I unfolded it from her clothes, and of her hands as they reached for my hardness; her hairy wetness as I touched it; our thrusting together, and her quick pleasure. She was the wife of a friend, and this one hasty act, done in her own house on a suburban afternoon while her husband was at his office, was all that we were to learn together of our bodies. I saw her only once more, at a large dinner the next night, held as a farewell to me, but as I sailed off I thought of her, a lively animal concealed inside her manners and clothes. In the loneliness of a soldier's life I repeated in my mind again and again, ritualistically, each of the events of our furtive meeting, and used the memory of them for a soldier's purpose.

The women with whom we normally sought our excitement in the city, often paying them for it, knew how to remind us at once, even in a public place, that there were bodies beneath their clothes; their gestures could quickly arouse my own body. But even though this could lead to an oblivion of thought or a reminder of common animality, the conclusion was sometimes merely a re-assertion of self-consciousness, pleasant, but contrived and solitary, as if the alien body lying beneath me were not really there. Even when a body heaved with mine, there was no discovery: these women wore their bodies as a kind of concealment; there was nothing more they could take off. But with my friend's wife there had been an unwrapping that still left something to be found.

As late as my stay in the beach community, images of her remained with me. Then I seemed to tire of them, as if she had at last been thoroughly unwrapped and proved humdrum after all, and as I watched the children playing on the beach I imagined again the son the computers had told me about—not now, absurdly, as a man of fifty, but

141

as a child. As I grew more lonely in the gregariousness around me, I imagined my little son coming to me with trust, enchanting with an innocent smile. Going to sleep I imagined kissing him on the forehead, and waking the next day I imagined that it was he who had awakened me, anxious to display some new mimicry of what he saw about him. Walking along the beach, I would sometimes think that I was holding his hand.

And now I saw him—in decline, garrulous, unable to gain attention. Coming out of the building, he walked several paces behind his two younger colleagues, waiting on the pavement as if uncertain whether they wanted him to accompany them. One of them spoke to him, half playfully, half insultingly. When he attempted a pert answer it merely drew a pert response. Speaking quickly of preparations for some other way of advertising the brassiere (they evidently did not share my old comrade's optimism that the censors' minds could be changed), they appeared to be blaming my son for the episode of the quivering breast. They walked off together, cleansing themselves of responsibility, leaving their problems beside him on the pavement like a bundle of dirty clothes. I watched his eyes and lips tighten as he tried to recover his pride.

I was aware of millions of forms of activity infinitely busy in interconnecting rhythms, so crowded and complex that I cannot now describe how they sifted themselves into millions of patterns, sought out further connections, constantly seeking and reacting. My own comprehension flickered feebly, but in one brief moment of its illumination I wondered if I was about to be absorbed into an eternity of wisdom. Energy was offered up from its vast aggregation, sometimes millions of charges pulsating in common rhythms. I resolved to lend myself to this perfect form for ever. Then there was a storm of disorder. A desperate flapping of rhythms contested with other rhythms. After this catastrophe some sense of form returned, but in my increasing periods of self-awareness it was clear enough that this universe was merely some mechanical thing. Its patterns of connection might be as much false or evil as good; it was founded on chance and some kind of complex mathematics, not on wisdom. Yet, as with other failures, in its very complication and in its seeking there was something splendid about it. Perhaps it could be copied and made perfect. Perhaps it would remain itself, never perfect, but the only way we should ever guess at perfection.

I had, for a few moments, been made aware of a human brain. It was that of my son. Now my awareness was of his consciousness. As he drove off in his car thousands of sense impressions bombarded each other. This huge circus of sensation—jumbled, connected, jumbled—never integrated; sometimes it seemed to take on a shadowy coherence, then it would jangle into a hundred distractions at once, a continuity of discontinuity. Sometimes the forms of concentrated reason threw themselves above the other diversities, billowing into recognisable patterns, but these would soon drift off, or float into some other shape as if, having once appeared, everything must then disappear. Even his attempts at self-awareness were merely a particular kind of interruption in a flux of thousands of other interruptions. Life seemed a diversity of interruptions in which there was nothing but the interruptions themselves.

Flat hardness under the soles of his feet. Smooth roundness in the palms of his hands. Soft tightness across his knees. Wetness in his armpits. Dryness on his tongue. Coolness on his cheeks. Tightness in his belly. Warmth in his crutch. The sounds of other cars, coming, going. The sound of his car, steady. The cry of a child. The rattle of a cardboard box. Rustling of paper. Cigar smoke. Decomposing sweat. Judgements of speed and distance. Twelve o'clock. All this in a second, while in his head he also evoked the smell of formaldehyde, visualised a country road, sang a song (with the beat of another rhythm interrupting), felt both melancholy and angry, and formulated the words of a letter of resignation from his firm which the words of some half remembered conversation kept interrupting. A few seconds later he had forgotten the letter and was reconstructing a conversation with a typist, thinking of her thighs.

Some of what briefly drifted around in his mind was of significance, but in recording it I shall not attempt to convey the totality of his sense impressions. The very simultaneity made it impossible to evoke, and although words were part of his consciousness, they were not its whole language, nor even a substantial part of it.

Flickering on and off as he rode in his car, along with hundreds of other interacting interruptions, some set tableaux were re-enacted in his mind. The first was in a doctor's surgery. A sharp smell. The feel of a leather chair. A beating heart. An ashtray. A glass cabinet of gleaming instruments. A strong, hairy hand on the desk, tapping with a pencil. The doctor's eyes behind heavy bifocals. The doctor's voice. My son would be dead. Three months. Six months. This scene flicked in and out of his mind several times. Dead in six months. Another scene. He is walking down a street. It is sunny. Cars go by. A woman holds a baby by both hands, helping her walk. My son is pleased that he will die. He walks into a café and orders a coffee. Then, in a scene within a scene, he imagines his death. The smooth calmness of the sheet. The kind pressure of others' hands on his. The smell of flowers. The blue sky outside. The slow ebbing of the brain. This scene is lost in other interruptions. He is washing his hands. The water turns grimy and swirls away. He touches his face. It feels fresh where he touches it. He is in a laboratory, testing his own urine. He makes marks on a card. There is smoke in the sky. It is his body, burnt into eddying molecules. Then, as one trying to master a passage of music, he again

144

goes through the scene in the surgery, the scene in the street, the scene in the café, the scene of his imagined death. With these established, he recalls another scene. He stands in a child's bedroom—his youngest daughter's. He has told his wife that he is soon going to die. He kisses his sleeping daughter on the forehead. Tears are in his eyes as he examines her innocence.

He imagines a sheet of paper. His handwriting appears on it. Credit: shares, so much; insurance, so much; superannuation, so much. Pause. Accrued holiday pay, so much. Debit: Mortgage on house, so much; loan from insurance company, so much; bank overdraft, so much; money owing on car and domestic equipment, so much. When one total is taken from the other and an annual percentage of what is left is compared with his present earnings, images of hate flash at him.

He was not going to die. I did not realise till later that the scenes of his coming death were merely a fantasy that held consolations of escape until he did the accountancy of death. He was debased with self-pity.

A memory. A photographic studio. A blank white wall. Photographic equipment. Stage scenery. A woman posing in undergarments. She manipulates her breasts and her brassiere so that they take some perfect form. She laughs at the result. Her breasts quiver. My son walks up to her, points to one breast, cupping his hand into its shape and making his hand quiver. The woman practises making one breast tremble, very lightly, like a leaf in a faint breeze. My son's voice: "Shoot it twice. Once with a quiver and once without. Then *they* can make up their minds." Someone says: "They can never make up their minds." Someone else says: "What minds?"

The breast quivers.

A memorandum, never written. Words appear in it and disappear, as if dissolving into the paper. The beginning forms, and drifts off. The end is being written, then stops. In the jumble two sentences are clear: "In offering two shots—one of a still breast and one of a moving breast—I was merely offering alternatives. It was for the client to make the final decision." I DID NOT MAKE THE FINAL DECISION appears on the paper, in capital letters, underlined. For the rest of the day the words "I did not make the final decision" are flashed again and again through the other interruptions, acquiring an obsessive beat, demanding justice.

The memorandum is finished. The words cannot be seen, only the back of the writing-paper, held in two hands. The hands throw the memo on a desk and brush it to one side.

In his imagination my son is making a long speech. He feels excitedly coherent. The words do not come, but a sense of pattern is there, highly reasoned. The two younger men who had dismissed him outside my old comrade's offices are sitting in soft chairs. My son is sitting in a hard chair. They are not listening to his speech. One of them cuts in before the speech is finished: "Excuses for everything." Hands tear up a memo and crumple the pieces, playing with them until they are shredded. "Everything you touch seems to give trouble." I DID NOT MAKE THE FINAL DECISION. Anything you touch seems to give trouble. I DID NOT MAKE THE FINAL DECISION. Excuses for everything.

My son drives on, heading for home. Self-pity twirls in, expanding and contracting, thumping against his skull, disintegrating into imagined scenes that flash and fade. Desks. Chairs. Memos. Encounters in corridors. Sentences and phrases clashing together. *Scene:* Young men rebuke my son: to him they seem old men, fathers. *Scene:* He is being congratulated: young men smile at him: he feels their smile on his own lips: his advertisement is brilliant: the censor has passed it: they praise him: there is no crisis: they laugh together. *Scene:* He is happy, walking down a sunny street, about to die. He thinks: I DID NOT MAKE THE FINAL DECISION. THEY KNOW IT WASN'T MY FAULT. THEY JUST DON'T LIKE ME. The words repeat themselves, coming on and off the stage like a chorus line; then they huddle formlessly, and fade away. *Scene:* My old comrade's body lies on the floor, the neck spouting blood: the severed head is held up: there is a discharge of anger, pulsating outwards, then an incoherent sadness. *Scene:* It is night outside: my son sits at his desk: paper in front of him: pen in his hand: a numbness in his mind: nothing to write: the word "creative" tumbles, in and out, in and out, among the other interruptions: hope. *Memory:* The photographic studio: blank white wall: the woman's breast, undulating: quick pleasure: men smile at him: "really creative". *Scene:* A small boy grins as his parents applaud: their laughter goes. Words crawl back into my son's head: I DID NOT MAKE THE FINAL DECISION. He strikes at them. A fog of sadness. *Scene:* He is an old bald clown: people laugh. *Scene:* He is sitting alone in an office: on the memorandum the words stick to his fingers like glue. *Scene:* He runs down a corridor, pushed by terror: he apologises to someone: and then apologises again, smiling and afraid. He thinks of his children. *Scene:* An old bald clown laughs with fear. *Words:* Overdraft, so much; mortgage on house, so much, etc.

When he arrives home his body still gives the sensation of trembling although it is not trembling. He sits in his car as in a cage. Shadows cast blackness, then dissolve into other shadows. He gets out. A familiar door. A key. Faces. His two daughters. Talk. Laughter. Talk. Talk. He must go and do some work. Corridor. Desk. Chair. Paper. In tiredness and terror he imagines women's breasts, trying to convert them into an advertisement.

Two women in brassieres are talking to each other: as one talks the other mimes disbelief: they touch each other's brassieres: the disbeliever mimes increasing con-

147

viction. My son imagines their conversation and jots it down. Another scene: a fully clothed woman riding a horse across a desert: her clothes disappear except for her undergarments: he admires her hips, both pliant and firm: he sees only her breasts and her head, the breasts in a brassiere: her breasts disappear, leaving only the garment that gave them their perfect form: it is in a cardboard box: only the box can be seen, on the sand: not on the sand, but on a silver tray beneath a date palm. He returns to the conversation between the two women in brassieres, writing it out, changing it, writing it out again. He types some other words about brassieres, rearranging the words, rearranging them, rearranging them.

Lunch. His wife. His two daughters. Two of his sons. Others. Awareness of the room flashes faintly at the dark horizon of his sadness. He feels the coldness of a knife, the softness of butter. Blood in the meat. A laughing mouth. Teeth. Conversation swirls, without sense. The warm redness of wine. Pain at the front of his head. Dust in his eyes. He adds touches to his despair without really seeing it.

He is at his desk again, the paraphernalia of work around him. A bald clown. I DID NOT MAKE THE FINAL DECISION. He rearranges the desert scenes: the woman rides her horse: her clothes disappear except for her undergarments: he admires her breasts, encased in a brassiere, both pliant and firm: she is clothed again, standing beside her horse: a female courier gallops up: she hands over a dispatch box: no, it is a briefcase: the briefcase is opened: a cardboard box is pulled out: there is a brassiere inside it: the woman is on her horse: she is clothed: her clothes disappear except for her undergarments: she fades away: only the cardboard box can be seen, beside a lake in an oasis. He types out descriptions of these scenes, in capital letters, numbering them, down one side of the sheet of paper. On the other side he types out words to be uttered as the scenes are shown on film.

He imagines darkness: a faint phosphorescence materialises into a naked statue of a woman: now only the statue's face and neck are seen: it is alive: the eyes move: the whole woman is revealed: all the body is alive but it stands as still as stone: undergarments clothe its breasts and its middle: there is a cardboard box with the name of the undergarments on it. He types out descriptions of these scenes in capital letters.

Now he is scribbling out the words of a song. In his concentration there is at last a simplicity and a sense of peace. He spends a long time on the song, then types out its words alongside the descriptions of the scene he has imagined.

He compares one lot of typing with the other. *Scene:* He is lying back, reading his own words to a harem of women in undergarments; as they move around him, gesturing and posing, the words of his song possess his head; packages of garments of the kind they are wearing are stacked here and there; in one corner of the seraglio there is a shop where fully clothed women are buying garments. New words chirrup through the words of the song, destroying it . . . *multiway straps . . . cut-away armholes . . . long line nylon lace stretch bra with rigid straps . . . waistline girdle . . . pull-on corselette . . . stretch strap with back adjustment. . . .* He is reading a typed report: "Because of the imbalance of the sample with overweighting in the 18-25 age group, no valid conclusion can be drawn from the survey. However, a few points which were not previously considered important have come to light. . . ." He is reading another typed report. Words twitter and squawk . . . *overall marketing approach . . . point of sale . . . store promotion . . . company image . . . marketing rallies . . . the young market . . . consumer research . . . price positioning . . . brand leaders . . . prestige brand . . . closed carton-type backs . . . swing ticket.* . . . He begins typing again. OUTLINE OF CENTRAL

149

CREATIVE APPROACH.

When this is finished he looks out of the window. In the sunset, across the roofs, the sky is deep mauve and purple-black. As the sky darkens, his consciousness flickers out. He is asleep.

Discomfort in the arms and legs. Greyness. A feeling of peace. A woman's voice. He wakes up. Dinner. The same faces. Conversation bombards him. His nerves twitch and seize his body, creating pain to report it. The simple rhythm of his heart becomes a drum, the churnings of his stomach turn to pain, the presence of his back forms itself into a shape of aching, his skull is set alight with irritation. He sits at the table thinking of screams. I DID NOT MAKE THE FINAL DECISION. Pain turns to emptiness and then to dizziness. The table moves towards him. He holds to the sides of the chair. Quietness. He goes off to another room, sits alone in its darkness.

The electric light is on. His family is around him. They watch the filmed drama in the cabinet. Its narrative snatches at his interest, as if there is a part of him that craves story-telling as strongly as his lungs demand air. He gulps in the narrative, living on its exigencies, criticising them and despising them, but breathing more easily. His body is no longer an outline of pain. When the long narrative is concluded his family begins talking again. He hears parts of their conversation, then bursts out into it himself, telling anecdotes, making them laugh. He charges out among them irregularly, as in a series of sudden bold raids, but between each charge he retreats to the cave of his privacy, terrified by its shadows. Within these shadows he sees the shapes of young men miming out the inadequacies of the work he did in the afternoon: he sees his own baldness hurtling down on him like a smooth white rock.

In bed, disjointedly, he imagines the next afternoon. A secretary brings in a memorandum. He reads it. He has

150

been dismissed. He walks down a sunny street. I DID NOT MAKE THE FINAL DECISION. A strong, hairy hand on the desk. The blue sky outside. The smooth calmness of the sheet. He imagines his secretary in a brassiere: her breast quivers. He feels his wife's nipple between his lips. He imagines his secretary finish undressing: the triangle of hair, the buttocks. He feels with his hand between his wife's legs. She turns to him and caresses him. He feels her passion rise, and his. Gauging her passion exactly, he mounts her just before it spills over, then proceeds to stimulate it again, carefully, as if going through by drill movements the loading, laying and fixing of a heavy artillery piece, touching one part and then the next. When the gun again fires, shuddering in recoil, he joins it in salute. He rolls off and lies still.

He feels cleansed by his pleasure, but now there is another alarm. He cannot sleep. His body turns and turns, each limb irritating with its separate liveliness. He tells himself stories. He sleeps. His uneasy dreams scarcely take shape. He wakes. It is still night. He decides to resign. He acts out his resignation so comfortingly that he soon falls asleep again. He does not wake until morning, but then with a start, as if he had been interrupted in something. I DID NOT MAKE THE FINAL DECISION. His youngest daughter is beside him. He feels the smoothness of her cheek. His other daughter comes in and tells him about the dreams she has had.

Under the shower, he lovingly soaps his penis. At breakfast sensations leap at him from his newspaper; images seize him from the television screen; in the kitchen a transistor burbles. The road leaps into a highway and the highway sweeps him through its curves across a bridge: the blue of the harbour flashes across his consciousness and he is swallowed into the city.

The concept of upwardness in a lift. Of friendship in a smile. Of disgust in a smell. Of hardness under his feet.

151

Of roundness in a face. Of tightness at his waist. Of length in a corridor. Of rectangles: his door: the floor of his room: his desk: his blotter: a sheet of paper. He draws rectangles on the paper as he tells his secretary to cancel all his appointments. He cancels all the rectangles with crosses. He tells her what telephone calls he will receive. He is alone. He looks at the rectangle of his shut door, trying to hear whether the telephone is ringing outside. He listens to the silence of his own telephone. It will ring. Ring. Ring. Voices will come through it and insult him. Why is the door moving? Why has his secretary come in? To tell him that a voice wishes to mock him? He thanks her for the coffee.

He listens to the silence of his telephone. It will ring. I DID NOT MAKE THE FINAL DECISION. A voice will come through the telephone and insult him. He picks up the telephone. He tries to speak to one of the younger men of the day before. No one is there. He rings someone's assistant. A voice tells him that there is a message that everything has been arranged. What has been arranged? The voice says there is no other message. He rings a photographic studio, asking for one of the young men. There is a long wait. A voice tells him the young man is not available. The telephone is again silent. He takes out from a folder the advertisements he has prepared in such confusion in his house the day before. He hides them in his desk. A foetus, chopped by scissors, swirls down a lavatory bowl.

A black sense of disaster rolls over. He sees his house in ruins, burning; his furniture scattered and smashed; his daughters slaughtered in the street. The images are too diffuse to understand. There is financial calculation. His house has not been ransacked and burnt: it has been sold. He has been dismissed and now lives in a smaller house. His daughters have not been slaughtered: he merely spends less money on them. He trembles with failure and fear at

152

the thought that he should spend less money on his children. The fear dissolves into love as in his mind he parades his children before him: the two little girls and the younger two of his three sons. He reconstructs their faces, their movements, their voices: he will not think of his eldest son.

He feels grimy, evil, sweating as, with excited malevolence, he contemplates his own duplicity. His cleverness shines at him darkly: he twists schemes around, contemplates tricks, imagines deceits. *Scene:* A conference, chaired by my old comrade. Subject: the brassiere advertisement. The absent chief executive is blamed for the advertisement. My comrade listens quietly to my son, valuing his brilliance. *Scene:* A conference, chaired by my old comrade's rival, the chief executive. Subject: the brassiere advertisement. My comrade is blamed for the advertisement. The chief executive listens quietly to my son, valuing his brilliance. *Scene:* My old comrade is deposed. *Scene:* His rival is deposed. In either case there is advantage for my son. Quick dishonesties prickle him with pleasure; subtle calculations caress him. Half in fear, half in pleasure, his penis swells a little with delight. His eyes on the door, he undoes his trousers, to feel the flesh. He glances down in admiration. Quickly. He does up his trousers and for a while works at the papers on his desk.

The telephone seems to click. When will the voice come through it and insult him? He listens to its silence. I DID NOT MAKE THE FINAL DECISION. He admires his guilt. Then he glances at his conscience. He dreams of virtue. Visions of goodness float around him, beyond all realisation. He preens himself that he should have such visions. He bites at himself for his badness.

A friend comes in. My son at once boasts of his skill at the previous day's meeting with my old comrade. He retells his speeches, without describing their failure. They both begin shouting and laughing. They congratulate

153

themselves on their intelligence. They sketch out schemes for tricking everyone so that the business to which they belong will still prosper, whatever happens to either my comrade or his rival. Then they speak like exiles or prisoners. What is happening in the offices around them? What mistakes are all their colleagues making this morning? How can the company they work for survive in such hands? They gossip of the stupidity of some of its most important members.

Alone. He draws rectangles on a piece of paper and crosses them out. He thinks with hate of my old comrade. He sees him as an old fool, pushing, thoughtless, ignorant of the subtleties of existence. He imagines a speech. Phrases. Gestures. *The old men must go. . . . An iron will is not enough. . . . There must be intelligence, rationality, planning. . . .* Applause. He sees my old comrade reflected in a thousand of the idiocies of his generation, and he hates the whole generation. He is a young man, trapped in a room of mirrors: from them old men's faces jeer. Then he sees his own baldness hurtling down on him like a smooth white rock. The walls of the building in which he is trapped rustle and whisper. What are all those young men now saying about him? He listens to the silence of his telephone. A voice will come through it and insult him. He looks at the shut door. I DID NOT MAKE THE FINAL DECISION. His daughters slaughtered, his furniture smashed in the street.

He admires his own talents. He mourns the world's ignorance of them. He recalls lines of verse. He tries to recite a whole poem he once wrote. The words dissolve. He sees the title: "Lines to the Photograph of a Young Soldier, Killed in a Duel". He sees the photograph. It is of me, sent to his mother. He thinks of his white hair and bald scalp; he pinches the fat on his belly; then he admires the youth in the remembered photograph. He remembers scraps of paper, drafts, unfinished projects. He thinks

154

words: *I would not write merely to please people. So I make a clown of myself a dozen times a week.* He imagines his death. Empty. Unknown. Nothing done. He rustles into confusion, searching. There shines some sense of himself, what he really is, some sensation in the darkness, as if suddenly discovering in a box of rubbish some piquant old souvenir. It drops from his hand. It has gone. He knows what he is *not*. He is not all this rubbish. Again there is the sensation that he knows what he *is*. A distant light, a faint form. A sense of hope and goodness. He sees another photograph. Himself as a youth, confident, eyes raised towards a distant view. I DID NOT MAKE THE FINAL DECISION. He again grows anxious with duplicity.

He is waiting. The phone does not ring. He begins walking around his room. He sits in one armchair. In another. He looks out of the windows, down at the cars in the street. . . .

The sensation that I could experience his consciousness dissolved and instead I could see him again from the outside. I could sense that a computer was calling me, but for a few moments I willed it away. I looked at my son by the window, his scalp, his white hair, his look of wistful cunning (suggesting that he could not finally trust his own cleverness) , his thumb rubbing against his forefinger. In him I saw some wreckage of myself.

His office was larger and better furnished than I expected from what I had taken to be his menial position. A bar jutted out at one end of it; the desk was big; at the other end were several small tables and some easy chairs; the carpet was thick. In my last resistance against the computer I saw a letter on the desk: at its top was printed the name of his company, and beneath it the words *From the office of the chairman;* it was signed by my son. I saw the outside of the door that led into his suite. Lettered on it in gold was the word *Chairman*.

155

I had the sensation that it was one of the two computers that had conducted the initial interrogation. "Our general instructions are that the tests must be expedited," it said. "Your preliminary report and the cross-examination of you on it will be needed sooner than originally seemed necessary. Because of unexpected developments it is now a matter of urgency." It paused, then added: "So far as this particular test is concerned, its purpose is a quick exchange of dialogue. Keep your statements short. I shall do the same."

I asked what I was to talk about.

"The test is purely mechanical, but we have decided that it is better if you talk about something that interests you: it adds the reality of field conditions."

I asked if there was any information about the purpose of my mission.

"That is a matter which, although important to us all, and now unexpectedly urgent in our whole enterprise, is not within the scope of this test, nor indeed within our particular knowledge."

I said that I pitied my son as if he were still a child and I could speak to him gently and wisely and calm his fears; but, in honesty, I recognised that if I had known him as a little boy I might now despise him for not remaining the child I had known.

"Those words came through satisfactorily," said the computer. "For the sake of saying something for the purposes of the test I shall now comment on them. It is obvious that your pity for your son would be, roughly speaking, what we used to call *charity*, but only provided that it was accompanied by a similar recognition of a childlikeness in yourself; without that recognition it is merely one of the condescensions of vanity, a condition not unknown in parenthood, and one of its temptations. Nevertheless parenthood can be a reminder of what goodness there could be."

156

I said that my son seemed to have unmanned himself, partly by a fashionable avarice from which he took no pleasure, in which he had only a feeble and intermittent belief, and which he excused as an act of love for his children, although for all I knew it was an imposition on them and could certainly be better expressed as love itself. As a result he had become a jumpier creature than most of us, taking bribes more desperately and shaking more meanly at every threat. Not only was there no honorable purpose in it: there was not even a sensible purpose of convenience. His overt ambitions and his vanities were so much matters of fashion; at the same time his conscience, although ineffective as a prompting to action, was so effective as an echoing mockery of his actions that he could be said to live without *hope,* except for his fantasies of duplicity.

"Your bringing hope into it represents quick, neat thinking," said the computer, "and it shows that the test is working well. I had intended to be the one who brought hope into it."

I said that my son obviously lacked any kind of *faith* coherent enough to spring hope loose. Faith and hope had seemed to me to be so closely bound together that there should be just one word for both of them. Although each could seem to exist without the other—a faith without hope and a hope without faith—this might merely be playing with words in special pleading. Except in the case of lunatics or very simple persons, did speaking of hope without faith mean anything more than a hope based on what was considered to be a *false* faith? In the old terminology, to speak of faith without hope was to speak of an uncertain faith; this was also true of the new terminology —either that, or it meant that the faith was merely an impossible ambition. One should be careful to distinguish between hope and ambition.

Although the computer seemed to be trying to

interrupt I added that a strong ambition could destroy both hope and faith, except in very lucky circumstances. Perhaps it was more useful to see views of faith and hope as somewhat similar to the view of life as a work of art: for a man of faith perhaps the greatest of all hopes was that his faith would survive. The paradox was that although action and thought were impossible without faith and hope, they could nevertheless also be, as the Prince had suggested, faith's and hope's greatest enemies.

Certain that the computer was now trying to interrupt, I added: "I need not remind you that the questions of faith and hope are closely related to the Prince's concept of pride and freedom, just as the idea of charity is part of that sense of brotherhood of which the Prince speaks."

"What you say may or may not be true," said the computer, "but you are saying it at too great a length for the purpose of this test."

I said that it was a matter of practical inconvenience for my son that his love of duplicity was not accompanied by a confident and sustaining cynicism.

"His duplicity," said the computer, "is partly a child's playfulness, partly its vanity and fear, but his conscience acts against it. Duplicity is more effective when it is the *instrument* of conscience, not its enemy. To your son duplicity is a naughty boy's game, played for itself but given some justification by his feeble and contradictory ambitions, but it is a game at which his conscience catches him out, because he lacks the faith of cynicism."

I said that presumably what the computer meant was that a conscience, or part of it, might be evil. Was anything more than this meant by the idea of temptation?

"I cannot answer that question briefly," said the computer.

I said that if the conscience were shunned, pride— or faith and hope—was impossible and, beyond questions of mere caprice, so was freedom, the sense of making a decision. Deprived of the support of his conscience, a man must live in anguish, on his knees. But it was also true that the pride sustained by a strong conscience might be the pride of temptation; the question remained whether the promptings of an individual conscience were good or evil. Sometimes it might be better to stay on one's knees than to stand upright and confident in evil.

. . . the wheel of a motor-car was kicking off lights into the night. It was a white sports car, streaming along a glaring highway. The man at the wheel was sunburnt and rugged: the brown hair of the girl beside him was teased out in the wind. It was a clear winter night. A mirror mounted on the dashboard picked up the dazzle of the headlights from the car behind. Beside the mirror there was the product. . . .

. . . a diagram of some perfect form of organisation for convincing humanity of the perfection and the necessity of the product was beginning to form an intricate concept that shone with confidence. Many colours assembled, in circles, rectangles and squares, or as straight lines, curved lines, lines of dots, or broken lines. Arrowheads were attached to the lines. Inside the shapes, shadings formed. Words jumbled into the shapes, giving them meaning. Then words changed. Lines moved. Arrowheads fell off. Shapes melted . . .

. . . there was a faint gleam on the lightly running surf. Feet squelched on the wet sand. The product was held up in a woman's hand, triumphantly . . .

. . . the cards were ticked and crossed, categorising the reactions to the product of both believers and unbelievers. Thousands of emotions had been pressed into mathematics. The cards were offered to a machine. The machine contemplated them and gave its answer. Hands picked up the answer. Now the final mysteries of the product would be resolved. The answer went from one set of hands to the

159

next as sure as a password, but as meaningless . . .

. . . there were many packets of the product, all of the same kind, pressed together on shelves in a store. A woman took one of the packets from the shelf and talked of her love for it. She held it up . . .

. . . two men spoke of the sincerity of the product . . . a man and a woman spoke of the product as a conjuror's trick . . . the man and the woman opened it and the genie inside gestured dreams . . .

Developing and then disintegrating, assured and then nervous, these images and others passed through my consciousness. The minds of some of those who worked in the advertising agency of which my son was chairman were spinning in and out of my awareness, throwing up, as they thought of the products they were helping to sell, symbols of imagination or counter-images of reason. There were such contrasts in their approaches to the selling of the product that it might have seemed an irreconcilable contest between the imaginative and the reasoned, if it had not been that some of the acts of imagination were at once mounted with cunning calculation into a chart of elaborate justification, and some of the acts of reason were prompted almost entirely by an imagination seeking pure diagrams, as in a mosaic. At times it seemed that the images of imagination were assembled by calculation, like familiar and well-worn spare parts, and that the images of reason came from emotion, irrationally.

It occurred to me that if I could observe more of this, even if it were concerned with nothing more than selling packages of goods, I might learn much about the human talent for making patterns. Not caring whether the product sold or not, I could have concentrated on the habits of those who used their minds to such an unimportant purpose, knowing that probably little more could be expected from the minds of even those who were concerned with greater ambitions.

There was a slowing down. In one office, and then the next, collecting in a general excitement, groups gathered to gossip. News had come that my old comrade had lost his dispute with the censors. There was to be a meeting of his board of directors in which, it was rumoured, things would go badly for him and well for the chief executive. My old comrade might be dismissed from the firm he had founded. What most concerned the gossipers—to some as a pleasant curiosity, to others as a dark fear—was their own future. The fortunes of their advertising agency rested mainly on the work they did for my comrade's firm. They were speculating as to whether his downfall might also be theirs. If he were to go from his company, might not his victors, wishing to remove all sign of his influence, destroy whatever reminded them of him, and as part of this process take away from their advertising agency all the business my comrade had placed with it?

In each group of gossipers there was talk of my son, the chairman of their agency. In the manner of conversation, their talk progressed mainly by the mutual interruptions of secret purposes and the self-interruptions of crossed motives, but in all this confusion there seemed aggregates of attitudes. It was among those who knew him least that my son seemed most important. To most of these he was a statue cut from ice, cold, hard and clear; they admired him for the cleverness of his analysis, as compact as a crystal, and even more particularly for his skill in deceit, as if he were some prince among ruffians in a time of disorder, robbing the rich and disbursing treasure to his followers. Others seemed more loyal to the man who had recently taken over as managing director and was now the real controller of the agency. To them my son was already "the old chairman". Yesterday's ice was today's slush. They, too, saw him as a trickster, but as an old trickster who knew only old tricks. Others, already regretting the inconvenience of the new managing

161

director's innovations, seemed to have fashioned out of some encouraging shadows in their own minds a kindly shape for my son: the old chairman was genial and sound at heart, interceding for the unfairly treated and saving them from the injustices of the new man.

The two younger men of the day before were sitting in an office as large as my son's but with newer and different furnishing. The one sitting at the desk, who from the conversation appeared to be the managing director, was short and thin, as if his body was too mean to grow large. His almond eyes and long brown hair gave him an air of reflectiveness, but he jabbed with words as he spoke of my son. Why had the old fool sat alone in his room all day? What mischief was he planning now? The other man, a little older, pale-faced and bespectacled, replied carefully, like one who knew his master for the day but kept an open mind on who would be his master tomorrow. He told how he had been talking to my son's secretary—the other interrupted to boast of the information she gave them—who had said that my son had taken no phone calls, nor made any; he had spoken to only one person, and he had eaten lunch at his desk. They discussed whether one of them should go in and try to deceive him into telling them what he was up to.

Then they began to curse him, as if by exorcism to drive him out, repeating to each other what they already knew. One of them said that all the interfering old fool had to do after he had been made chairman was to pocket his money and take it easy. The other spoke of the greed that had made my son accept the financial settlement they had offered him and the deceit with which he had then broken his bargain that he would leave the running of the agency to them. The first said that my son was supposed to be now simply part of their company's scheme of interior decoration. Yet, said the other, he had continued to interfere in the affairs of the company, with such intricate deceitfulness that he might be destroying it. The first spoke with special scorn of my son's vanity in pretending to be able still to contrive advertisements and the subterfuges by which he had taken credit for the work of others. The other complained of the childishness with which in derogating the work of his younger colleagues, my son was prepared even to threaten the reputation of the agency.

They were silent. Their curses had not driven out my son's presence. They began to speak of him with greater generosity, as merely one rogue among many, but an amusing one; they reminded each other with admiration of his trickeries, and laughed at the memory of some of his most remarkable dishonesties.

Another joined them. Like murderers re-enacting their crime to assure themselves that it has happened, all three began recalling their defeat of my son—the threats and enticements by which they had made him yield the power of his managing directorship and retire into the chairmanship, the intervention on their side of the larger company that owned their agency. They began to elaborate the hope that the circumstances of his earlier rise to office as managing director there might provide the grounds for removing my son altogether. They recalled these circumstances: the friendship of my son's cuckolded but legal father with my old comrade: the use of this friendship to gain for their advertising agency much of the business of my old comrade's firm: the credit that had come to my son from this: and the managing directorship of the agency that had also come of it. They examined in these accidents the advantage for themselves: some of my old comrade's enemies on his board of directors were their friends: it had been their agreed policy to befriend his rivals while my son continued friendly with my old comrade: but if my old comrade went, then couldn't they also get rid of my son?

Another came in with the news that, according to my

son's secretary, my son had, earlier in the afternoon, taken a call from my old comrade's rival, the chief executive. Their confidence drained as they contemplated the shiftiness of their own expediencies and the possible strength of my son's. Why was he speaking to his patron's enemy?

The telephone rang. It was one of their informants. My old comrade had lost the support of all but one of his directors and he had walked out of the meeting, which was now adjourned.

The sun's red inflamed the sky behind the blackness of tall buildings and the smoking chimney stacks of the powerhouse. The water ran black and red and the ships at the wharves sparkled with tiny lights. Holding a drink, my son stood on the balcony of his office while my old comrade shouted at him, his face sometimes as black and red as the river, sometimes blue and green from the flashing of the neon sign. He swore at my son for his disloyalty and ingratitude and accused him of betrayal; my son's intervention against him, he said, had lost him his last support. Mad with anger and envy, he screamed revenge, boasting that he would bring down all his enemies at once. My son spoke softly of misunderstandings and false accusations and quietly recalled old friendships. The sky was dark and the water black. Now flashing only with blue and green, my old comrade continued to shout at my son who, from the darkness, gave quiet, precise replies.

CHAPTER 12

the last interrogation

The computer spoke peremptorily. The time for tests and fooling around had ended, it said. Nor was there time to waste on further general speculation. There had been some setback to the Prince's fortunes and although it was a matter that would no doubt end with the Prince's triumph, there was no time for complacent dawdling. I must make my report at once.

When I asked what I was to report on, the computer said it had assumed that I had not gone on such an important mission for the Prince at such a critical stage of his glorious career without asking him why I was to go. Although the computer tried to bully me into some reply, I said nothing.

The computer now changed to a more leisurely, even coaxing manner. Surely, it said, there would be no harm in my offering something or other as an interim report? At worst I would simply appear stupid if well-intentioned, but from the reprimands I would receive I would probably sense the kind of report I was in fact expected to give. In any case, even if my report was so urgently required, perhaps no one would read it. Perhaps a report was needed simply to make up a file. Even if someone did read it he might simply pick out of it a few sentences here and there and use them to a quite different purpose.

I said that existence was not like a book. There was not necessarily a message or a summing-up at the end, and even if there were, would it necessarily be better or more significant than what had occurred before? If I were to speak seriously I must re-examine the many reflections I had made in my fifty years on the beaches, in my three adventures, and on my return to Earth. I would need time to think. The computer said that I was not at this moment required to speak seriously, or to think: I was required to make a report.

In explaining why I could not do so, I said that the observations I had made on my mission had so far been limited to small parts of the worlds of my old comrade and my son. In these particular observations of mine there had been no evidence—at least none that I could for the moment remember—that goodness in any way existed; yet from such narrow experience I would not necessarily come to this as a general conclusion. Although I had found no goodness, perhaps if I thought about it longer I might do so: perhaps we expect too much of goodness: perhaps we take the humanity out of it: perhaps we look for it in the wrong way and cannot see what there is of it.

"You are being long-winded about the inadequacies of your observations," said the computer, "but fashionably so. Most reports now begin like this, so you might very well leave all of that in as a preface. We shall turn that into the first section of your report and put it on a different-coloured paper: the heading will discourage a man of action from wasting his time in reading it, but it will be there nevertheless, and if you are challenged in some of your findings you can always point to this opening section as a face-saver." After a pause the computer said: "I advise you now to dictate to me a quick, businesslike section with some positive recommendations. For instance,

166

why not advise the Prince on the likely efficacy of some of his new slogans?"

Once again, I said, it would be ridiculous for me to reach any general conclusions on such slight evidence, but it had begun to occur to me that the idea of brotherhood —in some of its forms—could be overdone. It might have been misleading, for instance, for me to have made so much of the kind of brotherhood I had experienced with my companions after we had stormed the wrong beach and then had to make the best of it. There had been a nobility in our relations, but it was a nobility of desperation, perhaps akin to the sense of brotherhood of those who had believed that the world itself was about to end. It was not usual for such a clear sense of peril to exist, and although, as I had observed in the second of my adventures, it was often an act of statecraft to simulate or exaggerate danger so that men might act like brothers, it seemed wicked to do so, even if the result was sometimes good. Perhaps some of the violence of the rhetoric of brotherhood depended too much on a sense of catastrophe, making it seem possible that all goodness would disappear if some particular cause were not served. Some of the expectations of the Prince that we should have a universal pride in our species might depend too much on metaphor: at a time of peril, when some group we belong to is threatened, we might be able to take pride in a collective immortality transcending individual death, but a sense of immediate peril cannot be maintained indefinitely. In any case, it is hatred or fear of one section of the species for another that is usually most successful in engendering the sense of peril that inspires brotherhood: yet this kind of brotherhood is the most notable enemy of a universal faith in the whole species. Perhaps it was wrong to concern oneself at all with collective purposes rather than with the possibility of goodness as a relation between individuals, or as a quality within them. Otherwise we were left with the paradox

167

that while the manifestations of brotherhood could inspire some of our most noble aspirations, these aspirations were most likely to be put into practice when, collectively, we acted at our meanest and most unbrotherly.

"That will be enough on brotherhood," said the computer. "We shall give it the sub-heading *(i) Brotherhood* and underline it. Now give us something to put under the sub-heading *(ii) Pride and Freedom.*"

I said that these ideas were not only the Prince's, they had also been my own; that this conjunction appeared to have been the cause of my present predicament. I would now like to make some quick qualification of them. I saw no reason to change my belief that action (or freedom) was impossible without the hope that came from pride (or faith) ; but in itself was this belief anything more than an outline of a therapeutic technique? Must we applaud action or freedom merely for its own sake as if we were automata of which the only test was that we should continuously twist and jump? If we must, then we should praise my old comrade, whose pride made him free to jump in directions of his choosing although the faith on which he acted was despicable.

"In what you say you have been to some extent critical of the Prince's slogan," said the computer. "Perhaps you do this out of stupidity or vanity. Perhaps you do it out of bravery. But it is also possible that you do it out of calculation. Perhaps you realise as I do—I have been for so long a receiver of reports that I know everything about them—that it is not necessarily prudent to deliver back to a great man what you can remember as having been his thoughts when you last saw him: in the meantime he may have changed his mind."

I said that I had several things to add. In the first place I had not rejected the ideal of brotherhood; I had merely recognised the difficulties and dangers that came if its rhetoric took too much from that of war or other

168

catastrophes. The brotherhood I now believed in was something more gentle—more like the idea of charity as I had discussed it with an earlier computer, and in this there was not only pride but also humility. We should not despise ourselves for not being what we cannot be; neither should we take too much pleasure in it; we should recognise in ourselves the humanity we saw in others; it might be bad; it might be good; but we should acknowledge our shared condition. I added that there was doubt as to whether we needed the concept of brotherhood if we had the concept of charity, just as there was doubt that if we thought long about faith and hope we needed the new concept of pride and freedom. Even with some scepticism and humility, faith could prompt action. In short, I concluded, I was no longer sure whether we needed these new words the Prince had given us.

"If that were so," said the computer, "what point would there be in the whole rebellion of the Prince? Why should we all be going to so much trouble?"

I replied that it was not unknown for a rebellion to occur for reasons other than those announced; in any case, to give new meaning to old words was often the principal substance of revolt.

"That is a good answer," said the computer. "I shall delete the first part of it, of course, but I shall place the second part of it up higher, as a cautionary paragraph introducing the whole section. If we left it as an end piece it might not be noticed, and that could be serious for you."

When I said that something else was troubling me the computer replied that this suited its purpose: there should be several sections to a report and so far, apart from the preface, I had provided only one, even if it fell into three parts and was introduced by a cautionary sentence.

I said that I now saw, with something like agony, how little relation to the conduct of affairs there might be in what I had said, or the Prince had said, or anyone else had said, in the way of providing precepts for action. Were the workings of the human brain in any way related to our aspirations of how thought should go on? Or was there no relation at all between our aspirations towards thought and the jumpiness of the brain, its continuing, distracting bombardments, its feebleness, its turning on and off, its vindictive self-interest, its mirage-like qualities, and the distortions that came from the lying conventions of the senses that, second by second, mislead the brain like faithless courtiers? In the same way, was there any relation at all between our aspirations for the conduct of affairs and the actual practice of politics? Wasn't politics less a conflict between ideas than a conflict between men, and therefore day to day, and necessarily, little more—or nothing more —than a childlike shoving and pushing and seizing of advantages? It has been said that a great statesman must be a lion in boldness, a fox in cunning, and a pelican in selflessness and wisdom. But what if there are no pelicans, only lions and foxes—and eagles, vultures, snakes, mice, bears, and rats?

The computer said that the heading he would give to this section of my report was *2. GRAVE DOUBTS*. He asked if I had something more positive to say. I had raised possibilities, but what were my recommendations? If I could make any, they would provide a third section under the heading of *3. PROPOSALS*.

There was little more I could say, except to put in my own terms some of what had already been said to me by the illusionist and the story-teller: that faith itself might be as much an illusion as the evidence of our senses, but that this was a risk we must simply bear; and that despite all the uncertainties of affairs we could at least seize on circumstances to set a good example, even if only in failure. There was perhaps something more. Even if, as the Prince had half-suggested, there was something in the condition of our political behaviour that necessarily turned even

170

the wise and the good into fools and rogues, nevertheless faith demanded that this was a risk some must still take. Whether or not any good could come of it, we could believe that it might.

There was one more matter: hope was as good a guide to probability as fear; with hope and with a belief in goodness, even if of a modest and sceptical kind, it was possible to imagine that our species might slowly be improving itself. Perhaps none of our ideals would be realised in the forms in which we expressed them, but even if part of them could be realised in some other form, and even if this was largely by accident and in paradox, there seemed a chance of improvement: to be more positive, there seemed evidence that in many ways we had improved. Whether this was so or not, if all hope and all ideals were to be destroyed, what chance would there be that we should ever become better?

"I shall break that statement into four sections," said the computer. *"(i) Confirmation of the hypothesis of the illusionist, (ii) Confirmation of the hypothesis of the story-teller, (iii) Confirmation of the hypothesis of the Prince, (iv) Personal conclusion."* The computer paused. "On second thoughts," it said, "I shall make the reference to the Prince the first section and re-number the others accordingly."

When I said that the wording of these headings was more positive than the substance of what I had said— "confirmation" was far too strong a word—the computer replied that it was the purpose of headings and sub-headings to attract or repel the attention of a busy man; the sub-headings it had suggested might be so attractive that no one would bother to read what was written under them; on the other hand, if the hypotheses referred to were no longer in fashion, I could always point to the highly qualified nature of the substance of my remarks as an indication of my dissatisfaction with the hypotheses. The computer then suggested that there could be one more section of the report: *4. SPECIAL PROBLEMS OF THE MODERN AGE.*

When I replied that it was even more ridiculous for me to comment on this matter than it was to have spoken of the other matters, the computer suggested that the heading should be altered to read: *4. A FEW TENTATIVE PRELIMINARY OBSERVATIONS ON THE PROBLEMS OF THE MODERN AGE.* "It is not as good a heading as the first," said the computer, "but we must get on with this and finish it."

I said that there was one special problem among the kind of people I had observed (and I could speak of no one else). This was not so much a lack of faith, or perhaps even of honour, but a certain dowdiness of belief. A faith in money as the calculus of good and a sense of honour in profit still seemed strong in them, yet this kind of avarice, perhaps understandable in the poverty of the past, no longer made complete sense in what seemed the prosperity of the present. There were in all ages jumpy, cunning creatures like my son, and bold brutes like my old comrade, but in ages with a sense of faith and honour that circumstances made convincing, their crimes could have appeared more principled. Now they could seem merely silly. What seemed to concern the Prince was that the present age needed a new rhetoric of honour. Times had changed and rhetoric should change with them. The faith of emulation and the honour of conflict could no longer really be believed in communities where there was enough prosperity for all to share and enough skill and intelligence for prosperity to continue to increase (its increase perhaps hampered mainly by those who struggled with each other in the name of prosperity). No doubt conflict would go on, whatever the rhetoric, but this was no reason for not changing the rhetoric; to do so might do good. It was obvious enough to me that there should be a return to

172

some kind of rhetoric of *love,* although there was the danger, of course, that this could again excuse the violence it had previously aroused. If such a change occurred, there might at least again be a relevant sense of the heroic, and although it was the heroism of martyrs that had previously best served this cause, there could also be a boldness in prudence. I recognised, however, that there would be political difficulties if the Prince raised the banner of love as his cause, even if the word were given a more careful and limited or even sceptical meaning that made it little more than, as it were, a practical extension of the sense of charity. At the same time it should be pointed out that it was not unknown in politics to put oneself forward as the true exponent of what one had previously opposed.

The computer said that I had provided enough for a report, too much in fact, and that if there had been no urgency it might have gone over what I had said and, for my own sake, suggested some deletions.

CHAPTER 13

the unicorn

A low surf was breaking far out and then again close to the beach, separating the dull blue of the ocean from the olive green of the shallow water which in the swell sometimes seemed to turn itself inside out into a membrane of pale, glistening grey. Most of the surfers drifted up and down like seaweed near the beach; a smaller group floated farther out. Two headlands of light brown stone jutted into the sea.

Face down, face up, bodies lay on the white sand. A shrivelled old man ran to the water. Bums burst out of women's swimming-suits; breasts stuck up to the sky; thighs shook, navels winked. A woman's fingers felt her own fatness —arms, belly, neck—then leant over a man's skinny body and touched his back. Children's legs entwined; toes slowly dug into the sand. A hairy chest swelled out; strong hands rubbed the bigness of a rib carriage. Arms and legs flailed. Hands patted a woman's rump. The body of a young man lay on its back; the eyes were shut, and beneath the swim-suit the penis was erect. It was my body.

The dark eyes opened and swivelled around their clown's nose to look at the young woman whose hand rested on the thigh. I saw the lips pull down in a selfconscious

174

and cocky smirk—I had seen this often in photographs of myself—and then the face fell into a kind of stupefied wistfulness, the mouth sloppy and the eyes untrusting. Hands patted the woman's. At first the voice seemed not to be mine, but as it came back I recognised it, despite the strangeness that made it sound as if it had changed while it had been away. The body shifted in the sand; an arm went up into the air and bent over the woman's face, pressing down on her nose. At the end of the arms were the small fingers of which I had always been ashamed, and the thin wrist. There was a tattoo on the wrist, a thing I had never had. The design was made up of a name inscribed in a bracelet of nettles. It was my grandson's name.

My grandson asked the woman to describe his smell. He told her that during his weekend vow of poverty and chastity he would not wash. He wanted to lose shame for his body's odours, and understand something of them. When the woman said he smelt like hay he took her arm and rubbed it on his unshaven cheek, assuring her he would smell sharper than that before long. He lay on his back again, asking the woman to rest her hand on his thigh. His long hair and the light whiskers on his lips and chin made him look something like my grandfather as he had seemed in a painting done when he was a young man, dandified and dissolute, looking out at me as if inquiring whether I knew anything that he didn't.

He was telling the woman of some of the sensations of his body on the previous night before he had fallen asleep on the beach, and of how he would return there to sleep tonight. He described a sudden droplet of cold sweat from an armpit striking the side of his chest; the movement, one by one, of bones, ligaments and muscles as he called their names and demanded their salutes; the feeling, just before sleep defeated him, that he was a seesaw, tilting up and down. He asked the woman to make her

175

fingertips tremble on his thigh, urging her to extreme gentleness. He softly described to her his sensations as his penis again slowly became erect. When it was very hard he told her to keep her hand still. He shut his eyes and said he was thinking of her. He put a towel around himself and stood up, saying that his vow of chastity for the weekend meant that he must attend to such matters himself, but that he would be faithful to her in his imaginings. He kissed her hand before leaving her. In a cubicle in the dressing-sheds, where the green cement walls seemed to sweat salt water and where he smelt the sand on other men's feet and heard their talking, he sat naked, admiring his thighs, the short, curly hairs, and the blood-filled club that reached up to his belly. Then he caressed himself with his thin fingers.

The little red car swooped along the roads, up and down through hills and valleys of red-roofed houses, past small cemeteries of shops. My grandson explained to the young woman that he had asked her to drive the car because he interpreted his two-day vow of chastity to include an abstention from labour, and that she must pay for the petrol so that he could also keep his vow of poverty. The car shot past the contrived countryside of a golf course, coming out on the other side of a ridge where the houses were bigger and there were more trees. They raced another car to the top of a hill from which there flashed an image of the broad waters of the harbour and some of its bays. They roared along a twisting road so quickly that, with its trees and palms and rock gardens of flowers, it seemed like a wooded slope in which the houses were white boulders. The water flashed again several times, its light shining across lawns and through the trees of parks. They swept down a hill, past two huge orange cement-mixers slowly churning like cows, and then towards a steep-sided valley of houses that sheltered a little bay, the last before the harbour broke out into the ocean.

Pigeons ate bread on the promenade near the tables while seagulls stood quite still on the yellow sand. White dinghies were turned upside-down on the beach; yachts lay at anchor. A tiny boat with a blue sail drifted across the flat water; a launch glided silently towards the pier. A boy was bailing out a boat and at one end of the beach a man was pounding an octopus on the rocks. At the table where others had joined my grandson and the young woman, they were eating oysters and talking of burning flesh. It was children's flesh that obsessed them, black and red from fire bombs used in some war to which my country-men had sent troops. The flesh crackled and hissed in my grandson's mind. It was almost as if he hungered for it as food, although his words suggested that he considered the war the most terrible in history. Again explaining his brief vow of poverty, he had put an empty plate before himself on the table, describing it as his begging bowl and with much laughter demanding contributions to it. In the end he had more oysters than anyone else.

His consciousness kicked inside me like an embryo's legs. I had already felt its force in the dressing-sheds, when I shared his pleasure, and now I felt the violence of its images of horror—the bright blood, the explosions—and its images of excitement, as strong as his pleasure in the dressing-sheds though of a different order—slogans, police-men with batons, fists, kicking legs—and the thrill of taking risks in which he might get caught out. His excite-ment became mine, then it ebbed out of me, leaving me debauched. Clouds had drained the sky, and the water shone with a bright grey sheen. Distant across the harbour, the towers of the city poked up; against the dark trees of a foreshore, an aircraft carrier passed, grey gliding through darker grey.

Burnt crisp as a child's skin, fillets of fish now lay in my grandson's plate. He held out his right hand so that

177

his companions could see the tattoo of nettles on his wrist
with his name in them. He explained that he had had it
done so that he would know who he was. He shook his
wrist. The green and red of the nettles jumped. They were
talking, with great idealism, of violence as an expression
of creativity, and then, with great violence, of ideals of a
brotherhood born in struggle. My grandson held out his
plate to one of his friends who was eating crab. He was given
a large claw, its red shell cracked so that the white flesh
showed through. They spoke of a magazine; one of them
passed around some photographs that were to be printed
in it. An old woman lay on a stretcher, a hole blown
through her cheek and one side of her nose frizzled; a
child displayed a leg whose flesh had been hacked to the
shinbone; the body of a man, burnt black like a stick, lay
in a ditch; another body, naked and bleeding, was pressed
face down into mud. My consciousness was again pulled
into my grandson's. Waves of rage pushed me forward,
scepticism sucked me back. Currents of reason spun in a
whirlpool, shooting up as anger congealed in wit. The sails
of yachts had sprouted in clusters across the harbour. On
a pier at one end of the bay some men were hoisting up a
large shark; it hung by a rope from a crossbeam, its big
mouth open in the grin of death. Its executioner stood
before it, posing.

At my grandson's table they were drinking coffee.
Employing some jest, he had prompted one of them to
buy him a cake. He complained of the stinginess of his
father, and they began putting together some sort of
satirical sketch for their magazine, mocking the maladies
of their fellow countrymen, for which they had a cure so
simple and well known to them that no one bothered to
state it. His consciousness again became mine. When I was
again free of it, although still stung by its prickliness, and
while they were talking of some disturbance that was to
occur in the city that afternoon as part of their cure of its

178

sicknesses I contemplated more calmly what had already occurred to me in confusion: that there was in my grandson something of my own cast of mind at the time of my enlistment. The trivial objects of our ambitions were different—for instance, I sought excitement in war and he in opposition to it—but the ambitions themselves had similar shapes, although his, jumping around in contradiction, seemed more real than the ordered ones of my memory. There was the same desire for reason and the sense of self to be engulfed by action and the sense of comradeship—and the same immediate recoil against the possibility of this happening. He was prompted towards heroism as much as I had been; both of us were indifferent to the calculations of a man like his father, my son; yet we both reflected the odiousness of a man like my old comrade, brave lad of the trenches and chairman of a whorehouse for women. There were other things about this grandson—some merely stupid, some evil, and all of them, as the story-teller would have put it, childlike—which had never been part of my recognition of myself, but I now saw that they might be as much part of me as they were of him. I fumbled in an unfamiliar darkness of shame to find some new mirror for my conscience. Perhaps my whole conception of myself was false. A sail thudded. The water had darkened, glistening, almost black, but despite its darkening, things seemed clearer; the haze had gone from the headlands and on the pier the white paint glittered.

Stunted trees stood among the moss of the art gallery's Japanese garden room; water ran down one of the walls and flowed through white pebbles into a pipe that took it under the floor. Their backs turned to the paintings in the room, men and women, drinking wine, stood in a half circle facing my son, listening to him. His face was honest with laughter at his own wit. In a corner two men spoke

179

softly of his cunning. My grandson approached him, and father and son went into a private room and closed the door. My grandson shouted; my son spoke carefully and quietly. A glass pipe that reticulated the water of the fountain, curving into the room as part of its decoration, gurgled slightly, so that whenever there was a pause in the conversation it was as if the room's stomach rumbled. My son was ordering my grandson to come to a party he was to throw that night; my grandson was to dress in conventional clothes; he was to wash; as a concession he could, when it was over, go back to the beach for the rest of the night. They each threw into this squabble all their fanciful imaginings of what they were. My grandson in his mind high-stepped with boldness and pride like a sensitive and courageous pony; my son cantered with the cautious strength of an old charger. I was so buffeted by their visions of themselves—so much more grand than the issues they were disputing—that I did not notice the settlement. Instead I felt shame at the blindness which had damaged their love, perhaps so greatly that it might now appear only in the middle of the night, in memory, or when one of them died. Then I was dragged into my son's consciousness and knew nothing but a sense of great wrongs being boldly righted. Only when I was released again did I remember that the great wrong was a matter of going to a party.

In one of the main rooms of the gallery, people were pressing around the painting that was the sensation of the exhibition. Some of them seemed to be in fancy dress, others in various forms of conventional clothing; indeed, they provided between them a history of human costume. The large canvas before them looked like a medieval painting of a garden in paradise, except at the edges: here the colours were confused, only beginning to take form, but strong enough to suggest horrible monsters coming into creation out of the canvas, rearing up without knowing what they would look like. Within these unsure edges the painting was precise, but none of the animals in the garden was stylised in innocence. All that was seen of the lamb was its arse, pellets of dung clinging to the wool, maggots feeding in a sore on one leg. The lion was old, his mangy coat slashed in a fight, his teeth gone. The deer were rutting, their sharp feet tearing the grass down to the red earth. The fox was caught in a trap, kicking feebly, near death. Although painted with careful detail, these and the other animals were so small that from a distance they seemed to be done conventionally: their animality was apparent only from close up. They were painted without disgust, so that there could be pity in the contemplation of them. Disproportionately large, and taking up the whole centre of the canvas, was a human with pure white skin and the perfect proportions of a classical statue. Its posture, however, was that of a prancing unicorn. This representation of our species was both chaste and fanciful: between its thighs instead of genitals there hung a silver bell; gold bracelets grew from the bones of its ankles and wrists. The grace and purity of its form lay in the trunk of its body and in its limbs, but the delicate white-skinned hands, traced with little blue veins, dripped with blood and the face was mottled red, grotesque, clownish. The scalp and brainpan were translucent, showing the intricate inter-wrappings of the brain, but towards the forehead the wrinkles coarsened; they were stuck with hairs and trans-fused with pink. From the forehead there rose not a horn but a penis, white curving upward into red. The face, and also the penis, was that of my grandson, who was now posturing in front of the painting, for which he had modelled, projecting his hand from his forehead, the tattoo on his wrist swelling with the blood in his veins. He was mocking the picture as belonging to some earlier fashion.

In the gallery's white-walled courtyard, among clumps of statuary, a group of young people were discussing whether one of them, a woman, would take off her clothes and run naked through the gallery. My grandson came up to them and asked them to describe his smell. They spoke the words they might write on the courtyard walls, then discussed the absurdities of the other visitors to the exhibition. They drained their glasses in a mock toast and smashed them on the tiled floor. The tiles glistened with rain and the air was cool: the grey sky was still.

The little red car twisted through one of the older parts of the city, past terraces of two-storeyed white houses, then became jammed in a stream of bigger cars, stopping and starting in streets of restaurants and small hotels. Two of my grandson's friends were in the back of the car; he sat beside the woman who was driving. They drove slowly down a long sloping road, straight towards the scarlet sunset, then tilted away beside a park that became suddenly dark as its lights went on. They drove into the main part of the city where high buildings sparkled with lights. They parked in a back street.

The square between the tall black buildings glittered with light. On a raised courtyard there was a flourish of flagstaffs around a black fountain. Across the square a classical portico shone in flood-lights before a large park where pretentious palms stood up against the sky. My grandson and his friends were among those who struggled against the police on the courtyard steps, heaving up as the police thrust down. Banners of cardboard were held up and torn away. Kicking like hooked fish, young men and women were carried to the police trucks. Several young people broke through the police and scurried across the courtyard towards the black building where an entrance hall, itself several storeys high, jutted out into the courtyard, blazing with light. Policemen ran after them, others towards them. I gave in to my grandson's excitement. White shirts heaved against blue. Backs pressed against chests.

The courtyard was held by an enemy, and it was our task to take it.

Each light in the building shattered into circles of yellow sparkles surrounding centres of bright whiteness; then all was black. The computer had seized my consciousness more brutally than before. It shrieked at me. I asked it to repeat what it had said. It began again. It was giving some general warning of danger to the Prince and his followers. I implored it to be silent. Shame had overcome me from seeing so much of myself in my grandson, I said. I wished to look at my own silliness for a while, privately, and then to make some report on it. The computer blared back at me as impersonally as the address system of a military camp and with as much distortion: I could understand no more than that all the supporters of the Prince's cause were being called to show their loyalty to him in his present danger; but the appeal was expressed in such terms that even if it had been intelligible I could not have understood it. I shut off the noise and said I wished to make a confession.

After a while another computer broke in. It said that with so many messages going out at once there were bound to be some technical faults. It wanted to know what problem I had found in transmission. When I explained that I wished to contemplate my own showy childishness it asked me if I might not postpone such a consideration until there was less traffic on the line. Could I not in the meantime console myself by assisting the great cause of brotherhood and freedom served by the Prince? I replied that I could not answer until I had thought a little more about myself.

I was troubled, I said, by the possibility that my conception of myself might be altogether false. I had some picture of myself as something of a hero. This was, of course, a criticism, since I now recognised the baseness of so much of the heroic (although I also recognised the inadequacy of the alternatives), but it had now occurred to me that I might merely be a clown and all my self-criticism pomposity clothing folly. The computer reminded me that its function was merely to attend to the technicalities of transmission difficulties.

Another computer broke in. The records, it said, showed that at other times I seemed to have understood that complete self-recognition was unlikely and that one could act on supposition rather than on certainty. Surely I still knew that if one tried to devote oneself entirely to self-knowledge it would restrict other activity to the point where—as in certain other experiments—what was being observed (this also raised, of course, the insoluble question of who or what was doing the observing) would become oversimplified and any conclusion reached would be likely to be misleading. Retreat into a wilderness for the purpose of self-observation was, it said, merely to observe oneself in the particular circumstances of a wilderness.

Another computer broke in: "It is not possible to stop altogether being a fool. Surely it is enough to contemplate the possibility of sometimes achieving wisdom?"

The previous computer then asked me to be silent while another computer transmitted two service messages. After a pause, a new computer said: "I am to inform you that the Prince's present setback is unquestionably of only a passing nature, that the loyalty of his supporters still sustains his noble mind, and that fidelity to his cause will ensure that, after so many vicissitudes, his glorious designs will triumph." A pause, and then: "I am further to inform you that at two-thirty tomorrow morning, by which time the Prince will again be victorious, there will be a communication to you—perhaps from the Prince himself—of the nature of your own earthly mission."

It was my son's house late at night. Food lay in plates, abandoned glasses stood half-empty. The house was littered

184

and its air stale, but the party guests clung to it, most of them excited or stupefied from the alcohol that had passed into their blood from their stomachs, some of the others from a more fashionable drug that had passed into their blood from their lungs. Disordered consciousnesses leapt out in the bold companionship of laughter or anger, or smiled sleepily within themselves. In a back room some of the younger guests laughed at the lack of voguishness of those who preferred to drink a drug rather than smoke it, while in one of the large rooms some older people spoke of the immorality of those who chose to smoke a drug rather than drink it. Washed, and dressed in conventional clothes, my grandson smiled with indifference at an old woman whose thin, sullen face was pecking towards him with insulting questions. In another room, my son, his face sad, bored two patient young men with his wit. My old comrade was also there. With the confidence of a cannibal chieftain he was commanding a wide circle that had formed around him.

The senses of being of all three of them seemed to call out to me. I resisted. There was some subtle purpose to my son's party, but I did not care to discover it; I preferred to imagine that I was sitting through a play in which I had lost interest. In two hours I would know what I was to do and who I was to be; either this or, if by then the Prince had proved to have failed in his adventure, there would be the excitement of receiving new orders from his victors, or of being their victim. Whatever happened would probably take me away from people such as my son, my grandson, my comrade. But despite my indulgent speculations, I was dragged in and out of the consciousness of all three.

As my son made failed jokes to his guests a silence cut off his mind from what he was saying, as if he were part of his own bored audience. Tousled thoughts and troubled images flickered through the bright and secret part of himself—so much busier than the part that was jerking away in the darkness of others. Scenes of his disloyalty to my old comrade cut into him with flashes of self-righteousness as, hero-slaying villain, he jumped about on his stage. Surrounding him, supporting him, throwing him into the air, carrying him in his triumph, were my old comrade's enemies. Then my old comrade staggered on, bleeding but still alive. One by one the dancers turned to him, slowly joining together and lifting him up in triumph, jeering at my now discarded son. But my son played the suppliant: he threw out his arms and wriggled face-down on the floor until he was generously beckoned by my old comrade to join him. Soon both of them were carried in triumph on the backs of the others. My son felt hot with love for my old comrade, caressing his biceps through the cloth of his jacket and feeling the bones and skin of his hand. Had he not invited him to his party? Had they not been joking just now?

As my grandson smiled at the old woman he wondered if her pubic hairs were white. His mind rested inside its cave, dozing, good-humoured, lazily interested in the shadows on the wall. The surface of the room, the pallid paintings, the woman's red lips, her skinny fingers, were each of them things to look at, but what was the connection between them? Within the dark cave, the white bones of his violence lay piled up. Something was scrawled on the wall —a policeman threatening a coward. My grandson imagined his fingers curled in white hairs. An orange cushion stared at him. Yellow curtains stood up stiffly. A policeman had threatened him and he had run away. The lobes of the woman's ears were pink.

My old comrade's brain quivered with trumpet calls. His imagination jumped on the smooth wood of his board-room table. He took out his pride and played with it until, swollen stiff, it throbbed the rest of his awareness away. Outwardly he was telling yet another story of his commercial boldness; inwardly he told himself, again and again, that they could do what they liked with the firm he had sold but *(rat-tat-tat!)* he would remain as its governing director. He would gulp down their insults to feed his honour. They could not take that table away. He had fought for it and won it. Down the table he saw the faces looking up at him. He saw himself telling them of the evils and waywardness of my son. He began to prepare his revenge.

It was the largest of the rooms, and the emptiest. Music came into it, and talk and laughter from other rooms. My old comrade, my son and my grandson were before some windows, together. On one side my comrade reared up from a chair, face red, belly panting, cigar ash on his jacket. Drink spilling from his glass, head jerking with defiance, he roared out a song. My son curled his feet under his chair. His face pointed like a hunting dog's; his thumb rubbed his forefinger; he smiled beneath dark eyes, his brows set wistfully. My grandson stood between them and stared at them as if he were both their prisoner and their conqueror. He gave his hand a flick, and the fingers jerked stiff. He touched the tattoo on his wrist with his other hand, and then, pressing his wrist against his forehead, he moved the fingers up and down, waving them and smiling to himself.

The thin bare poles of the yacht's masts sliced the sky. Across the dark water of the harbour, lights shone from high buildings. The red car shot out into a wide road flaring with advertising signs; car lamps flashed red and white up a slope towards tall buildings which seemed ablaze with orange. The car swivelled into a turning and drove through dark valleys and hills of unlit houses. Near a crossing, on a cleared space, dozens of empty motor-cars were flood-lit; carnival lights were strung above them. The car went down a long hill and swept in a wide arc along a beach, stopping in the centre of a long, curving promenade.

My grandson got out of the car with a young woman

187

and a young man, both of them yellow-haired. They stood arguing beside an oil stain on the concrete road, their feet among crushed cardboard cartons and discarded fruit skins. The promenade stretched the whole length of the beach. With its three layers of concrete roads, its high walls, its concourses and sweeps of cement steps, it was its own world of yellow light separated from a valley of dark houses and blobs of blue street-lights by a long, low cement building, and from the black ocean by sand which in the light had turned pale grey.

My grandson left his two companions and walked across the beach towards the rocks of one of the headlands. When they had driven off, he walked back to the cement wall that divided beach from promenade, lay down on the dappled sand, and fell asleep. However sullen, even in sleep, and however puffed out by dissipation, his face seemed so young that for a moment I forgot his follies. One arm stretched out, showing the tattoo that gave his body, otherwise the same as mine, its special brand. I thought of how I had once been trapped in the body of which this seemed an almost perfect copy, and of the tricks that body had played, so different from the aspirations I had held for it. As I looked at it, it seemed a shed skin, part of the rubbish of the beach. If ever there were to be more punishment, for me it would be to be trapped in that body again.

The time had come for the message from the computers, or from the Prince. I searched outwards in my mind, using the tricks the computers had taught me, but I did not even feel the echo of their will resisting mine. I thought of the Prince himself, hoping by this means that I might summon his message. But no message came. I thought of the story-teller, the illusionist, the young conspirator, constructing each of them in my mind in turn, and throwing words at their images, pleading for their intercession. There was no answer. I again tried to summon the sensation that I was talking to a computer. There was no reply. I tried again to imagine the Prince. There was no answer. I remembered another trick the computers had taught me, and tried it. Only my own words came to me. I tried once again to think of the Prince, attempting by some means I could not understand to reach him, if he had not abandoned me. But there was no answer. I went back to the most simple tricks the computers had taught me, and failed. Then I tried to drain my consciousness of all striving, to make it an empty vessel for receiving the message, if there was to be one and if the Prince and his forces had not been vanquished. To clear my mind I contemplated the round moon and the wide empty greyness of the beach. A flat surf was running. White foam was breaking in a black sea.

the prisoner

It was dark in front of the tall black building. I was moving through the air, strong arms holding me. When they put me down in the courtyard I was shaking with cold. Vomit scalded my mouth . . . They brought me naked before a prince who was holding inquiries in the green cement dressing-sheds. When they showed him my thin hands, sweating salt water, he declared on my guilt . . . In the back of the police truck as it drove away from the black building the guards passed around photographs of the burnt flesh of children . . . A woman's curling white hair sprouted from the cloth of the orange cushion I was carrying among the tables of oyster-eaters, crying "Won't you buy my pretty poverty! Fresh chastity today!" and ringing a small silver bell plucked from my own groin.

Sweat struck my side. I could feel the stiffness in my bones and muscles and ligaments, and the sand on my hands and face. Eyes opened. I was still on the beach. Red streaked out across a dawn sky and the street lights shone pale on the headlands. My eyes closed. There was something I must do. Some message I must receive. Something had to be done. But there was no answer . . .

Now only the lights on the seesaw showed, tilting up

and down . . .

I was awake. An old man was running on the sand against the red part of the sky. Gulls rose. Several other old men ran down the beach to the pale glistening water. Wire rubbish-bins sprouted from the sand. There was no one else on the beach. Gulls strutted on gleaming pink. Tiny figures fished from the brown stone of the headlands. A man and a woman were bathing in their clothes.

My eyes closed again. There was some answer I must receive . . . I was overcome with the sensation of having a body. I smelt its foulness, felt its sticky tiredness within its clothes. Hair prickled my face and the back of my neck. My eyes opened. The water now was red and blue. Gulls screeched. I shut my eyes, feeling the flesh of eyelids press into the flesh of cheeks. My tongue tasted bitter, and my brain ached.

Eyes opened. The colour had gone from the pale sky. The red open car came down the promenade. The young man and the young woman with yellow hair got out of it and waved to me. I pressed down the soles of my feet into my socks, feeling their texture with my skin. There was a pain in one thigh. I stared at the round moon and its clear markings. A little cloud beneath it went red.

Clouds burst into pink throughout the sky. At its centre, across the blue ocean, the sky shone red, blue and grey. On the headland there was a children's playground and an aeroplane roared above it. The street lights went out.

A special redness flushed out at the point where the sun was now to appear.

The young man and the young woman walked along the beach towards me, calling out. I stretched my fingers towards them and saw on my wrist the tattooed bracelet of nettles, with the name on it.

In the spinning of the Earth the ocean dipped. An arc of crimson slid up above the blue.